THE SHADOW CITY

Five Elements
Book 1: The Emerald Tablet

THE SHADOW CITY

DAN JOLLEY

HARPER
An Imprint of HarperCollins*Publishers*

Typography by Torborg Davern

17 18 19 20 21   CG/LSCH   10 9 8 7 6 5 4 3 2 1

First Edition

For Tracy

Always.

PROLOGUE

The woman known to her followers as "Primus" stood on the roof of a tall building. From there she could see San Francisco, the bay, and the mountains all spread before her like a painting.

One day had passed since the battle against the child-elementalists on Alcatraz, and plumes of smoke still rose from the prison isle.

The police had shut down the island soon after the children had fled and the Eternal Dawn retreated. Perhaps the hapless authorities blamed the earthquake for the damage the confrontation had done to the old buildings. Maybe they believed the bursts of flame that had lit the sky had been from a gas leak.

Those without the Art could not see magick for what it was, and so their minds had to concoct ordinary explanations for the extraordinary events around them. They could never have guessed that the great wave that had leaped from the waters like a fist had been the product of arcane manipulation, or that the howls that had screeched across the water belonged to creatures ripped straight from another dimension.

Primus wondered how such ignorant minds would interpret the breach that the children had unwittingly opened on Alcatraz. To her, it looked like a crack of gold hanging in the air, but it was so much more. It was the makings of a doorway between here and Arcadia.

"Arcadia." Primus sighed into the cool wind. The realm of pure magick that waited just behind San Francisco. *The secret city that will remake the world.*

No longer draped in the ceremonial robes of the Dawn, Primus wore a nine-hundred-dollar suit that would have fit in at the most high-powered Wall Street offices. The breeze rippled her skirt, and she smoothed its fine fabric, grimacing as her hands grazed the bruises from her fight against the children. But this discomfort was slight compared to the pain of her defeat.

Her *failure.*

She paused for a moment to let the pain wash over her.

She had come *so close* to success. Mere *inches*! And this made her loss all the more bitter.

She would *not* fail again.

History was on her side. The Eternal Dawn had outlasted every last one of their foes. It had been over a century since the creation of Arcadia, and the cult had never been stronger. It had never been closer to remaking the world.

Yes, the battle of Alcatraz had been a setback, but success was just ahead. And the prize for victory was nothing less than an eternal dawn for all of humanity. To seal her place in this glorious history, all Primus needed was to find the descendant and the Emerald Tablet.

But how?

The Dawn's hunters prowled the streets and abyssal bats patrolled the skies, but of the children they'd found no sign.

The leadership of the Eternal Dawn was a heavy burden, and Primus had made her way to this quiet part of the city, to this peaceful rooftop, for a moment to herself. She gazed at the smoldering old prison across the water while she pondered her next move.

She felt a prickle of irritation at the sound of soft footsteps behind her. She assumed it was simply one of the building's residents, come to gawk at the scene at Alcatraz.

"I believe it was a gas explosion," she said, preempting the inevitable rubbernecker question.

"It was nothing of the sort."

Primus turned quickly—not so quickly as to look startled, but quickly nonetheless—and raised one skeptical eyebrow when she saw the speaker. "Oh? And what do *you* know about it?"

The speaker approached slowly. His eyes never left hers. Primus immediately saw something strange in those eyes. Something deep and dark and dangerous, and not of this world. "I know a great many things. I know the *Truth*. I know of the *Way* and the *Power*."

Primus's throat seized in shock at the familiar incantation of the Dawn.

Impossible!

The figure in front of her smiled. Slow, cold. Deadly. *"Dvai shvioutei pivuntxa, majia povrunshei taigho shviunta."*

"How— Where did you learn those words?"

He stepped closer. "I knew those words long before I came to know you, Charlotte."

Primus's heart felt as if it might rupture from pure astonishment. She fell to one knee and bowed her head. "Master . . . Master Thorne! I apologize. You are . . . changed. When did you return? *How* did—"

"To your feet," he commanded.

She stood, obedient. *Jonathan Thorne!* She clenched her hands into fists to keep them from trembling in his presence. She didn't know how he had crossed the void between worlds, but it was undeniably him. Power radiated from him. Standing in front of him, she felt like a child standing before a god.

"This is only a shard of myself. A fraction of my true might.

You must ready the proper rite to bring about my complete return." He circled around her as she spoke.

She kept her eyes on her feet but could feel his gaze carving into her back as he passed behind her. "We have begun the process already, Master."

"You have failed." He clipped his words off flatly. "I know of your past efforts, such as they were. Capturing the wrong sacrifice, releasing a null draak, letting the Emerald Tablet slip through your grasp . . ."

Primus reddened as the list of her errors lengthened.

"And I tell you," Thorne continued, "that even had you captured the true descendant, your efforts would have been in vain without the Tablet. My total self has passed beyond the confines of mere mortality. No simple exchange of blood for blood is sufficient to bring me whole to this world again. I am more than a man, and a greater sacrifice must be offered. The Tablet must be destroyed during the ceremony—its energy will be consumed to fuel my crossing."

Primus's head twitched involuntarily. For a moment she thought she had misheard. "M-Master? *Destroyed?* Sir, we *need* the Tablet! All that knowledge . . . all that power . . ."

Jonathan Thorne, founder of the Eternal Dawn, growled low in his throat. The sound emerged odd and eerie from the flesh vessel he was inhabiting, growing and deepening until Primus felt it in her bones. The sound consumed her consciousness, the words reverberating deep inside her mind. For a moment Primus feared she might pass out.

"I-I'm sorry, Master, I don't—"

"No, you do not understand, and there's the pity." He stopped in front of her and clamped her jaw in one hand, positioning her head so his eyes bored straight into hers. "We require a Book of Power, yes. But remember that everything in the universe casts a shadow, Ms. Terrington. *Everything.*"

Realization slowly dawned on her.

Everything casts a shadow! Of course!

As she processed the implications of this new knowledge, Thorne released her, strode to the edge of the roof, and looked across the steely water to the smoking prison.

"You will capture the descendant and bring me the Tablet, Charlotte." He clasped his hands behind his back, still as a stone as he gazed at the city. "You shall have your second chance. Your *final* chance. Do you understand?"

Primus nodded, mute with awe and terror.

"I won't disappoint you, Master! On my soul, I swear, the descendant and the Tablet will be yours!"

Thorne turned back to her. The Founder's gaze slashed through her like a blade.

"Good," he said. His voice was in her ear, and also in her mind. "Now listen, and remember, and *obey.* . . ."

1

"This'll just be a tremor, right? We don't need a full-on earthquake."

Kaz sighed. "Look, Gabe, if *you're* nervous about this, it's only going to make *me* nervous. And I *really* don't want to be any more nervous than I already am. So please. At least try to relax. Okay?"

Gabe put up his hands, backing off, and decided to stare at the Brookhaven Institute for Psychiatric Rehabilitation instead of at his friend. He'd never seen the hospital at night before. During the day the massive brick building could have passed for a hotel, but now its security patrols and chain-link fences topped with barbed wire made it look a lot more like a prison.

A few days ago, it would have seemed completely crazy to try to break into a place like this. But a lot had changed over the last few days. *And crazy or not, it's still good to be out of the tunnels we've been hiding in.*

"Those guards just turned the corner, so I'd say we have about four minutes," Lily said, stepping out from behind a hedge.

"Did the wind tell you that?" Gabe asked, just loud enough for Lily to hear him.

"No," Lily whispered back. "My eyes did."

Lily's twin brother, Brett, stood on her other side, their coal-black hair blending with the surrounding shadows. The three of them formed a half circle around Kaz as he knelt a few paces in front of them, speaking softly to himself. Kaz's fingers traced patterns over the ground in time with his words.

He'd been practicing this ritual for the last two days. It didn't make much sense to Gabe, but then he didn't expect it to. Earth was Kaz's element. Kaz spoke the language of dirt and rocks and sand, and he could bend the earth to his will.

Just like Lily could with air, and Brett with water. Just like Gabe himself could with fire.

Kaz's words grew louder, deeper. They echoed up from the ground below, filling with grit.

Gabe tried to relax but couldn't; for all he knew, Kaz using his elemental power might draw down a swarm of abyssal bats, the winged, skinless monstrosities that were scouring the city, searching for them.

"Keep an eye out for anything weird, guys," Gabe said.

"Weird?" Brett asked. "Like, skinless-eyeless-hunter weird? Or skinless-eyeless-dragon-thing weird? Oh, or like humorless-snotty-Ghost-Boy weird? So many flavors of weird to choose from."

"How about all-of-the-above weird," Gabe said. "Minus Ghost Boy, I guess." Jackson Wright seemed to be on their side, for the moment. "Seriously, though, we need to be on the look-out."

"Don't worry, man." Brett clapped Gabe on the back. "Any of those beasties shows up here and we'll be ready. Besides, we showed the Dawn who was boss back on Alcatraz, didn't we?"

The Dawn. The thought of the apocalyptic cult made Gabe shudder, partly in fear, but mostly in anger. He turned back to Brookhaven. This was where they'd first met Greta Jaeger. She'd tried to help them, and the Dawn had murdered her.

He squeezed his eyes shut, remembering her last moments. The image of an abyssal bat's daggerlike talons punching through Greta's back and out through her chest was like a horrifying GIF he couldn't close. He couldn't forget the icicle-sharp pain in her eyes . . . or the split-second when he and Greta both knew she was about to die. He'd never watched anyone die before, and he hoped he never would again.

Though given that the Eternal Dawn and their creatures were still hunting him and his friends, he didn't think that hope was very realistic.

Gabe peered into the shadows for the thousandth time, worried that he might find a member of the Dawn sneaking up on them. But the only person he saw was Jackson. The blond, pinch-faced Ghost Boy was leaning against a tree behind them, his arms folded across his chest and his usual sour expression on his face. *He still looks like a ghost, he's so pale.* That wasn't exactly accurate, since Jackson had never *technically* been a *ghost. But what else do you call somebody who gets stuck between worlds for a hundred years, and keeps walking through walls for a while even after he gets unstuck?*

Gabe *really* wished they didn't have to drag Jackson around with them, but he'd finally made peace with the knowledge that they needed him.

Gabe, Lily, Brett, and Kaz represented the four natural elements, but Jackson, for reasons Gabe still didn't understand completely, was bound to a fifth element. *Magick.* And if they were going to do what needed to be done, all five of them would have to work together.

Greta had told Gabe that with her last breath.

The fact that Jackson had tricked them, lied to them, and almost gotten them all killed multiple times in his effort to return to this world . . . well, they just had to deal with it.

"All right," Kaz said. "Showtime, I guess. Cross your fingers.

Actually, if you can, do me a favor and cross your toes, too."

"You got this, Kaz," Gabe said. He tried to sound more certain than he felt.

They'd gone over the game plan for getting into Brookhaven what felt like a million times. Gabe could still imagine too many ways it could go wrong. But they didn't have a choice.

His mom and his uncle Steve were trapped in Arcadia— and it was up to Gabe to rescue them and destroy the shadow city once and for all. He had no clue how to do this, but he *did* know that Uncle Steve and Greta had been working on plans to accomplish something similar for going on ten years. His best hope was that Greta had squirreled some of their research away in her room here at Brookhaven.

Kaz's fingers touched the ground. The tiniest of tremors ran through the earth.

"Just a little rumble," Gabe had said when he'd come up with his plan. "Make them think it's an aftershock from the quake a couple days ago. Just rattle things around enough that they evacuate the building."

Lily had nodded. "And then we make a mad dash to Greta's room and hope we find something that'll help us."

"Exactly."

The next tremor Kaz made was more noticeable. A nearby tree swayed, as if in a gentle breeze.

Brett held the Emerald Tablet in both hands. At first glance, it looked like a solid piece of green crystal, about the size and shape of an iPad. But it was actually a book, which opened to reveal thick pages covered with runes—glyphs that could only be read by someone attuned to one of the elements. Each of the elements had a different language, so the four of them each saw something different written in its pages.

As if the Tablet weren't weird enough already, it didn't cast a shadow. Gabe could see this peculiarity now, in the unblinking glare of the hospital's security floodlights. Without a shadow, the Tablet looked like it had been poorly photoshopped into Brett's hands, as if it were only half in this world.

The hairs on Gabe's arms bristled at the sight. *Creepy.*

Gabe wished he'd never seen the stupid book, but at the same time, the information it held might make them all better at their . . . Gabe still struggled with how to describe their elemental gifts. *Do we call them "powers"? Or does that make us sound too much like superheroes?*

Kaz's eyes had gone solid slate gray, and shimmers of green energy flashed and flared across their surface. He curled his hands into fists and thumped them into the grass. The ground beneath them buckled, knocking Lily off-balance and into Gabe.

The trees around them began swaying back and forth as if they were trying to shake free of their leaves. From inside the institute, the shrill buzzing of an earthquake alarm pierced the air.

That should do it. "Okay, Kaz," Gabe said. "I think we're good."

Car alarms started going off, one after another, up and down the street. Kaz kept his head down, both fists on the ground.

"Kaz, that's enough," Lily said.

Gabe felt something in the air around them . . . tighten, as if the entire world were clenching its muscles.

The street in front of them fractured and heaved with a sound like an avalanche, and on the other side of Brookhaven's chain-link fence, a wide, jagged crack zigzagged its way from the hospital's foundation all the way up to the roof.

Gabe shouted, "Kaz!" He grabbed his friend's shoulders and dragged him to his feet. Two fist-shaped craters remained in the ground where Kaz had been feeding his power into the earth.

"Sorry," Kaz gasped. His eyes flickered from gray back to brown. The green light sparked and died away. "Sorry."

A rumbling, cracking sound rolled out from the hospital, and Gabe saw one of its walls begin to buckle. He was afraid the whole building might come down, but after a few seconds, it looked as if it had settled.

"What the devil was that?" Jackson demanded, appearing at Gabe's side. "You were supposed to frighten the people out of the building, not entomb them."

Kaz's face fell. "I know, I know. I'm sorry, I'm really sorry.

I—the first tremors went totally right, but then there was this . . . like, this voice in my head . . ." He carefully ducked out of Gabe's grasp, as if Gabe's hands were so delicate that Kaz feared he might break them. "I didn't know how to stop it . . ."

A rush of sympathy filled Gabe, taking in Kaz's haunted expression. Gabe had heard a similar voice in his head before. More than once. The voice of fire, urging him to give in to the power of his element, urging him to greater and greater destruction, hissing for him to *burn . . . burn . . . burn . . .* What would earth tell Kaz? *Break . . . crush . . . shatter . . .*

Kaz put his hands out as if to steady himself. "It's gone now . . . I think. Yeah. Okay. I'm okay."

Their powers were incredibly useful, but they were also seriously dangerous. That on top of being hunted by the Eternal Dawn and their twisted creatures from Arcadia . . .

God, we are in so far over our heads.

"Well, it worked," Brett said drily. He pointed at the stream of inmates and employees rushing out of the building, shepherded along by scrub-wearing orderlies. They gathered on a patch of grass just shy of the perimeter fence.

The orderlies were wearing Tasers in belt holsters. Gabe remembered that most of the patients here had violent tendencies, and he felt a pang of unease. "Okay, the doors are open. Let's go. We don't know exactly how much time we're gonna have."

Brett said, "Sounds good to me." He eyed Kaz speculatively.

"If Aftershock McShakesalot here can keep himself in check."

"I *said* I was sorry." Kaz shoved his hands in his pockets and let his shoulders slump.

Gabe cleared his throat. "Let's keep moving. Brett, are you ready? Can you get us in without anybody noticing?"

Brett cracked his knuckles, all cocky grin and white teeth. "Watch and learn, my young apprentice!"

Gabe returned the grin. *Same old Brett.*

They crept through the shrubbery, skirting the confused crowd of anxious inmates and employees as they headed for the big fountain in front of the hospital.

"Okay," Brett said, glancing around, "stay close to me."

Brett closed his eyes, and a sheet of water flowed up and over the lip of the fountain. The water encircled all five of them and, between one heartbeat and the next, sprang up above their heads, containing them inside a hollow column. Gabe peered through the thin sheet of water at the near-perfect mirror of one of the institute's windows, and where their group stood he saw . . . nothing.

Through tricks of light and reflection, Brett's water column had rendered them invisible.

"Come on." Brett gestured toward the hospital's entrance, his eyes open again. "Keep together as you move, and don't touch the water."

Stepping carefully, they edged toward the door, and the column of water glided along with them, keeping them hidden.

Gabe had known what to expect, since Brett had been practicing this trick in the tunnels while Kaz worked on his "minor tremor" ritual, but seeing it in action? Gabe could barely believe it.

For a short time, Brett had been trapped in Arcadia, too—but Greta Jaeger had helped Gabe and his friends figure out how to rescue him. Brett had told them only bits and pieces about the time he'd spent in the dangerous, shadowy, magickal version of San Francisco. From what little Brett *had* said, the dark city sounded even worse and more bizarre than Gabe had imagined. His time there had left Brett more introspective, but it also seemed to have *focused* him. This water illusion was easily as slick as anything Gabe had seen Greta pull off, and she'd had decades more practice. It made Gabe wonder what he might eventually be capable of himself.

Once they were out of sight of the door, Brett let the water column fall. It left a sizable puddle on the floor, though not even a single drop splashed onto their feet.

Kaz scampered over to one of the computers at the front desk, looking up Greta's file. Peering over Kaz's shoulder, Gabe was glad to see that Brookhaven hadn't reassigned her room. They could only guess how much the hospital—or anyone else—knew about what had happened on Alcatraz two days ago.

"Got it," Kaz said. "Let's go. Elevators are this way."

Sweat glistened on Lily's forehead as she concentrated on the lock in Greta's door. Gabe peered over her shoulder. "Are you sure you can do this?"

She looked up at him with one raised eyebrow. "The next time we need a building burned down, you're our guy. But this takes finesse." Turning back to the lock, she added, "Now please. Let me work."

The air stirred around them as Lily's eyes turned silver-white. Listening hard, Gabe thought he could hear a series of tiny clicks from inside the barrel of the lock. Lily was right. This *did* need finesse. The best he could've done was melt the lock out of its bracket. Lily sighed and stood, eyes back to normal, smiling but a little shaky. "Go on in. It's open."

Lily and Brett both have me outclassed in the precision department. But Kaz's almost-out-of-control quake from earlier gave Gabe a tiny bit of perverse pleasure. *At least I'm not the only screw-up in the group.*

Brett led the way in. Each of them had a tiny flashlight—Jackson had all but worn out the battery in his, he'd played with it so much in the tunnels—and they directed the beams to the desk just inside the door.

Gabe wasn't sure what he'd been expecting, but he'd definitely been expecting *something*. Instead, the desk was bare, and the small bookshelf next to it stood empty. No papers, no books, definitely no journals detailing Greta Jaeger's research into the nature of Arcadia and the people trapped there.

Frustrated, Gabe was about to say a very rude word when Kaz sucked in a quick breath. The beam from Kaz's flashlight had swung over to the bed—and illuminated a human-shaped lump underneath the covers.

What the . . . ?

Goose bumps sprang up on Gabe's arms and ran down his spine. *Maybe the hospital* did *reassign Greta's room?* Had they missed whoever this was in the evacuation?

He sucked in a breath. *Or maybe it isn't a patient at all . . .*

Gabe raised his right hand, palm up. Energy from the electrical wiring sparked and crackled around him, and he drew it to him, drew it *into* him. A marble-sized ball of flame manifested in the air above his palm, ready to grow much larger if need be.

Lily was the first to move. Still silent, she crossed the room, took a deep breath, and grabbed the corner of the sheet. Before Gabe could say anything, she threw the covers back.

Greta Jaeger lay on her side on the bed, peacefully asleep. Illuminated by the flashlight beams, wisps of fine gray hair fell across her deeply lined face.

Lily jumped backward as if the older woman were a rattlesnake.

"It can't be." Gabe tried to keep his voice from quavering. "I saw her die! We all *saw her die!* It *can't* be!" But, oh, did he *want* it to be.

"You know that to be true as well as I do, Gabriel," Jackson said, striding forward. As he passed by, Jackson gave Gabe a brief but effective glare and murmured, "We were both right there when it happened, weren't we? I remember it *so very well.*"

Gabe's heart clenched in a pang of shame.

Back on Alcatraz, Gabe had tried to throw Jackson into the rift that led back to Arcadia. Greta had managed to stop him from making this terrible mistake, but that was what got her stabbed by an abyssal bat. If not for Gabe, Greta would still be alive, and Jackson knew it. The others had no idea, but Gabe wondered how long it would be before Ghost Boy decided to clue them all in.

Jackson prodded the sleeping figure in the shoulder with one stiff forefinger. "Old woman. Wake up."

Kaz said, "Hey! Show some respect!"

Jackson gave them all his favorite condescending smile. "I might. If this were a human." Jackson swirled one hand in the air, and pure, golden light—the visible manifestation of magick—lingered there, forming into a mosaic of glyphs. The glyphs dropped, glimmering, and sank into Greta Jaeger's body . . . which immediately turned translucent, shimmering with a bluish glow. The effect was ghastly. It looked like Greta's skin and shape were molded like magickal clay around a vaguely human-looking dummy.

Kaz and Lily both gasped. Brett just squinted, staring at the shape on the bed as if studying it.

"Who . . ." Lily swallowed and started again. "*What* is that?"

"I felt the magick coming off it as soon as we walked into the room." Jackson sniffed. "It's an *apographon*. The word is Latin, and it means 'copy' or 'replica.' I surmise Ms. Jaeger constructed it using her mastery of elemental water, though I cannot imagine water alone producing something so intricate."

Brett snorted but said nothing.

Gabe chewed on his lower lip. "Hey, Brett. If Greta hid any water glyphs around, do you think you could find them?"

Brett cocked his head. "I don't know. Let me give it a shot." He moved to the center of the room, closed his eyes, and slowly raised his hands. When he opened his eyes again, it was his turn to gasp.

"What?" Lily rushed to her brother. "What is it?"

Brett turned in a circle, mouth hanging open.

"*What?*" Lily demanded.

"There are glyphs *all over* the walls!"

Kaz said, "Yeah, but they're water glyphs, right? None of us can see those."

Jackson sighed. The condescension came through loud and clear. "Here," he drawled. "Allow me to pull the wool from your eyes." Jackson's own eyes shimmered and turned a solid, glowing gold.

The room came to life.

Column after column of waving, looping script covered the walls, flowing and surging as if in a current. Gabe couldn't actually understand the water glyphs, but just looking at them felt like dipping his feet into a cool, soothing stream.

Gabe couldn't deny some grudging respect for Jackson's magickal abilities. Not even Greta had known exactly what he could or couldn't do; Jackson and his ability to wield pure magick was unique. Gabe's nose wrinkled. *Yeah, and uniquely irritating.*

"So, what do all these say, Brett?" he asked. "Can you read them?"

Brett's eyebrows pulled together as he stared at the walls. "Yeah, I think so . . . give me a minute here . . ."

Lily jerked away. "Ew! Brett, did you just spit on me?"

"Huh?" Brett pulled himself away from the glyphs to look at her. "What? I did *not*."

"Oh yeah? Then why is my arm wet?" Lily held up the arm in question and shined her light on it.

And froze.

Gabe whispered, "Oh no."

It wasn't spit that had landed on Lily's arm. It was a glob of golden slime. The kind that coated the creatures sent by the Eternal Dawn.

Jackson's eyes flared gold again, and Kaz started swinging his flashlight wildly around the room as his voice rose to a near shriek. *"Where is it where is it where is it?"*

Gabe called up another ball of flame. If there was a hunter or an abyssal bat somewhere in here, it was about to get flash-fried. He froze in place when he saw something behind Lily.

Something that looked like . . . a tentacle?

Something coming down from the ceiling.

Gabe raised his hand toward the ceiling, expanding the fireball, and its dancing red-gold light illuminated a creature straight out of Gabe's most terrifying nightmares. With the shape of a manta ray and the tentacles of a giant squid, the creature was also partially camouflaged. Its color and texture mimicked the acoustic tiles that made up the ceiling. But the light from Gabe's fire stripped the camouflage away, revealing its skinless, gold-slime-covered body.

2

"There!" Gabe screamed. "On the ceiling!"

He was about to bathe the creature in flame when two of the tentacles lashed down, wrapped around Lily and Kaz, and yanked them flailing and screaming off their feet.

"Careful!" Brett barked in Gabe's ear. "You'll burn Kaz and Lily!"

Near the window, Jackson Wright had conjured a golden disk the size of a hubcap, and whenever a tentacle got too close, he used the disk like a shield to bash it away, his face a mask of mingled fear and hatred.

"Get me down!" Kaz gurgled. "It's *squishing* me!"

Lily might have been trying to talk, but one ooze-covered

tentacle had wrapped around her head, covering her mouth. Her eyes blazed silver, and wind whipped savagely around the room, but it had no effect on the creature and only made Gabe's eyes sting.

And the creature itself was growing larger. Its ray-like body made horrible squelching noises as it spread out across the ceiling, and one flap of slimy skin slapped down over the doorway, blocking it even as it darkened to match the grain of the door's wood.

Gabe struggled to keep focus. Brett was right—if he lost control, the way he had when he burned down the university building where Uncle Steve taught, he'd char Kaz and Lily to cinders. And maybe Brett and Jackson, too.

"Brett! Cut Kaz and Lily loose! Then I'll hit its body!"

Brett nodded, and the small sink in one corner of the room exploded into porcelain fragments as a stream of water as thick as Gabe's wrist shot out from the pipe. Brett guided it with deft motions of his hands, and the stream split in half and narrowed at the ends into blades like giant X-Acto knives.

The blades sliced through the tentacles holding Kaz and Lily—but two more tentacles grabbed them before they even hit the floor.

How many grabbers does this thing have? Gabe grimaced as he saw new ones emerge from the sheet of slime. *As many as it needs! Okay. Concentrate.*

Gabe jabbed his right index finger toward where he thought

the creature's brain would be. A beam of fire no broader than a pencil lanced up and carved easily through the creature's flesh, but the tissue around the point of impact closed like water around an oar.

"You're going to have to do some actual *damage*, Gabriel," Jackson shouted. "Why are you holding back?"

Gabe wanted to scream at Jackson, but he kept his voice to a frustrated growl. "Because I'm trying not to kill Kaz and Lily!"

From near the ceiling, dangling upside down from a repulsive tentacle, Kaz shouted, "Right! Yes! Good plan!"

Lily's mouth was free now. "Gabe! If you don't cook this thing, it's going to kill us anyway! Now *hit it*!"

Of course she was right. Struggling to still his mind and focus, Gabe dragged in electrical power from throughout the building, and his eyes became flaming, boiling suns. His voice came out like the roar of a blast furnace—"Get ready to hit the floor!"—and he unleashed twin spouts of flame from his hands that tore through the creature's body, blackening its flesh.

Kaz and Lily thumped to the floor. The creature, nearly burned in half, made a sound like a hissing scream and yanked all its tentacles back into itself. But it was still blocking the door.

Kaz stood, patting himself to check for injuries. "That was," he gasped, "*so gross*."

The creature stayed stuck to the ceiling, looking like a gigantic, badly overcooked fried egg. The stench of its burned body reached Gabe's nostrils. He wondered if anyone else could tell when he threw up in his mouth a little.

"Is that it?" Lily asked. "Is it dead?"

Gabe tried to figure out if it was breathing. Did a thing like this breathe in the first place?

"So. Are we just going to stand here until the orderlies come back?" Jackson asked.

"We still need to get what we came here for," Gabe said. "Brett, take another look at those glyphs. Greta must have written them for some—"

A sickening, slurping sound cut him off midsentence. He turned to see the smoking chunks of the creature's flesh snap back together, splattering all of them with golden ichor. Before he could react, at least a dozen new tentacles exploded from its edges.

Gabe would have been whipped across the room if not for the golden barrier that sprang up between him and the creature. Jackson stepped past him, hands raised to project the shield, golden eyes radiating power.

Jackson's barrier kept the tentacles momentarily at bay, but the creature quickly began oozing its way across the ceiling, expanding again as it headed toward them.

Kaz shouted, "Guys, we really, really, *really* need a way out of here!"

"I got the glyphs figured out!" Brett said. "I think! Let me try something!" He turned and focused his attention on the toilet. Immediately the water rose up out of the bowl, spinning and whirling, and became a liquid vortex easily five feet across. Brett shouted, "That's our exit!"

Gabe couldn't tell who looked more horrified, Jackson or Lily.

"Surely you jest," Jackson said.

Lily turned to face her brother. "Are you serious? You want to *flush* us?"

"It's a portal! A water portal! All the glyphs lead right to it! Just trust me!"

Brett's solution sounded good enough to Gabe. He had no doubt that the Eternal Dawn had left this God-awful mutant tentacle freak here in Greta's room as a trap, and he'd guided his friends right into it. "Anywhere has got to be better than here!"

Apparently overcoming his disgust, Jackson took a running leap and dived into the vortex. It didn't look as if he'd slid down into the toilet; more like he'd just *disappeared*.

He wasn't the only thing that vanished; so did the barrier that had been keeping the creature's limbs in check. Gabe's eyes ignited, and the tentacles jerked back as he fanned them with flames.

"Go, go, go!" Brett's eyes glimmered the deep blue-green of the ocean. "I'd really like to slam the door on this thing!"

Lily nodded and jumped in.

"Kaz, what are you doing?" Gabe asked. Instead of making for the vortex, Kaz was scampering back toward the bed.

"I'll be right behind you," Kaz shouted over his shoulder.

"Burn it hard and jump!" Brett screamed at Gabe.

Gabe grunted agreement. One last burst of flame made the beast scream and writhe, and while it recoiled, Gabe dived into the vortex.

To Gabe, it felt like going down a gigantic waterslide, the kind where he'd whip down the tubes so fast it'd make his swim trunks ride all the way up to his shoulders. At the end of a slide like that he'd expect to crash into a huge pool of water. But plummeting through the vortex, Gabe couldn't tell where or even *if* it would end. The vibrations all around him threatened to shake his teeth loose.

Then Gabe burst out of the portal, soaked to the skin, and slammed down butt-first onto a hard floor with an impact that made him feel like his skull might pop off his neck. Hands grabbed his ankles and dragged him out of the way—that was Lily, he saw, blinking water out of his eyes. He felt Kaz crash into him.

Out of the corner of his eye, Gabe saw Kaz skid across the floor and careen into a wall. Then he turned to look at the watery vortex that churned and swirled on the ceiling just in time to see Brett pop out. Instead of crashing down like Gabe and Kaz, Brett landed nimbly on his feet. He grinned down at Gabe, who was still sprawled on the floor. "Nice landing, dude." Brett stuck out his hand to help Gabe up.

From near his head, Gabe heard Lily say, "Where are we?"

But Gabe, still staring past Brett at the vortex on the ceiling, screamed, "Look out!" as five familiar, slimy tentacles shot through the portal and reached for them, writhing.

Brett slammed his hands together. The portal snapped shut, severing the tentacles, and Gabe scrambled backward as they flopped and spasmed around the floor, flinging gobbets of golden slime everywhere.

After a few moments of slime-slinging, the tentacles stopped moving. Gabe took Lily's hand, and she hoisted him to his feet. He glanced around and spotted Kaz and Jackson off to one side by some armchairs. Neither one looked hurt, though Kaz was so tense his shoulders were practically level with his ears.

Staring at the inert tentacles, Kaz said, "I really hate that thing."

"Hold still a second," Brett said. He closed his eyes and moved his hands in little swirls, and every drop of water abruptly slid off Gabe and puddled around his feet. The same thing happened to Kaz, Lily, and Jackson. Brett himself was already bone-dry.

Lily ran a hand through her hair, gazing at her brother. "I could've done that with air, y'know." She grinned.

Brett flashed a grin right back. "I think you mean *you're welcome*."

"Yes, that was quite a feat." Jackson sniffed disdainfully. "You two would be quite popular at a public swimming hole, I have no doubt."

The vortex was closed, the creature was gone, but Gabe still couldn't look anyone in the eye. "Guys . . . I am *so* sorry. I led you right into that trap. Just walked us all straight into it. That was totally my fault."

"Hey." Lily poked him in the chest with a stiff finger. "Look at me." Gabe raised his head. Lily said, "I don't remember you holding a gun to any of our heads. We're in this together. Right?" When he didn't answer, she got louder. *"Right?"*

"Right."

"Right. So quit it. We all need to focus."

Gabe glanced around at Kaz and Brett, who both nodded, so Gabe didn't push it. He still wanted to punch himself in the face, though.

"Hey—uh . . . Brett?" Kaz said. "Thanks for getting us away from the giant snot creature, but . . . where did you *take* us?"

Brett shrugged. "No idea. But I figured if Greta set up all those water glyphs to activate a portal, it had to lead somewhere safe."

Gabe took in his surroundings. The floor he'd slammed into was smooth parquet, and judging by the floor-to-ceiling bookshelves that took up three of the four walls, they were in someone's private library. *And a nice one, at that.* Or at least it had been nice, before they arrived and got water and Arcadian creature goo all over the place. *Uncle Steve would have loved a place like this,* Gabe thought. It reminded him of Uncle Steve's office in the house they'd shared—though this was way fancier, and the books on the shelves looked even older.

The light coming through the few tall windows was too dim for Gabe to read any of the books' titles. Gabe spotted a floor lamp next to a chair in a shadowy corner. "Let's see if the power's on." He crossed to the lamp, found the pull chain, and tugged on it, and he almost jumped straight out of his skin when he realized someone was *crouched on the floor by the chair*. Gabe backpedaled away from the figure and didn't *quite* fall on his butt again as he babbled, *"Whuh, whuh, what is that?"*

Because it wasn't a person by the chair. It was some kind of creepy mannequin.

Kaz stepped up beside him, peering at the crouched figure. "Holy fish sticks. I didn't see that coming."

Gabe spun toward him, his heart rate very gradually climbing down off the ceiling. "What? Didn't see what coming?"

"Well . . ." Kaz swallowed. "When I picked it up, back there in the hospital room, it still looked like Greta."

Gabe scowled. He didn't even know who or what he was scowling at. It just felt right to scowl as he turned to examine the weird thing. With its magick stripped away, it was a roughly human-shaped construct, made of gray stone, slumped under the light of the floor lamp like an oversize marionette with its strings cut. "You brought it with you? *Why?*"

Kaz said, "I felt bad just leaving Greta back there asleep—I mean, *fake* Greta—so I just . . . y'know . . . grabbed her."

Jackson walked over, Brett and Lily right behind him. "It's a kind of golem, I surmise." Jackson peered at it, his eyes flickering to gold and back again. "A skeleton, if you will, around which Greta Jaeger built her apographon—her copy. The illusion would have been completed with a water skin." He started to say something else but broke off in the middle of a word. There was a funny look on Ghost Boy's face as he went to one of the windows, all of which bore heavy, old-fashioned toile curtains. In fact, it seemed to be the curtains themselves that he was interested in, not the window or what might lie beyond.

Gabe watched Jackson sourly. *Weirdo.*

Kaz nodded slowly. "So if Greta had that, uh, *toilet portal* set up, and used it to sneak out . . . she would've needed something to cover for her while she was gone. Right? And that's where Fake Greta comes in? Orderlies do a bed check, and they see her in there, and they're like, 'Everything's good.'"

Lily gestured at the hundreds, maybe thousands, of books on the shelves. "So would that make this place . . . like, her *lair*?" She moved closer to the golem and reached out to touch it, but seemed to think better of that idea. "I wonder how often she sneaked out?"

"She might have taken off whenever she felt like it," Gabe said.

Lily stepped around the golem and went to another window, ignoring Jackson, who had begun turning slowly in place, staring into every corner of the room. She moved the curtains and peered outside. "I think we're in Nob Hill. Like, one of the town houses."

Without another word or even a glance, Jackson walked out of the room. Lily called, "Where are you going?" But he didn't respond. "Jackson! You're acting weirder than usual! You okay?"

Still no answer.

"Well," Kaz said, watching Jackson disappear down the dimly lit hallway, "should we go after him?"

"He's probably just hypnotized by a bottle of Windex or something," Gabe said. "Back to Greta—if she kept leaving the hospital to come here, I'm betting this is where she kept all her research. We need to learn as much about this place as we can. So step one, I'd say, is seeing if we can spot any more glyphs. Okay? If Ghost Boy wants to wander around with his nose in the air, let him."

"Yeah," Brett said, "sounds good to me."

Gabe grinned. "I'll go first."

Gabe took a deep breath and let his eyes blur. Slowly, carefully, he reached out with his fire sense, seeking sources of energy. The electricity humming along the wires of the house called to him, practically sang to him. For a few heartbeats he could *see* the power flowing through the home's copper veins, blue-white fiery lifeblood just waiting to be used.

But no glyphs.

"Sorry, guys. No fire writing anywhere. Kaz?"

Kaz did the same, and with the same result. "Nope.

Nothing. Place is built on some *fantastic* bedrock, but no earth glyphs."

They turned to look at Lily. She closed her eyes and concentrated, and when she opened them again they had turned solid, radiant silver—a brilliant, beautiful shade that made Gabe's insides tingle.

She gasped. "Whoa. Jackpot."

"What is it?" Brett touched her shoulder. "What do you see?"

Lily turned in a slow circle. "Air glyphs. They're *everywhere*. Walls, floor, ceiling, windows. Gabe, they're just like the ones we saw at your house."

Gabe frowned. His house had been all but destroyed in an Eternal Dawn attack, and a big part of the damage had been caused by air glyph booby traps left by his uncle. *Wait—what? Does that mean Uncle Steve was here? He was Greta's friend . . . But when would he have come?*

Brett seemed to understand what Gabe was thinking. "Guess Dr. Conway still has a few more secrets."

Feeling hollow, Gabe nodded. "A few. Yeah." Gabe suddenly missed his uncle with a sharp, hot pain. The last time they'd spoken, Gabe had been screaming at him about his nonsense occult research and his arbitrary rules. But his research hadn't been nonsense at all, and the whole time, Uncle Steve had been fighting to make sure Gabe was safe. *What else don't I know?*

"Well." Gabe cleared his throat. "At least none of the air glyphs have, y'know, *gone off* yet. Guess we're not considered hostile, huh?"

Brett scanned the room, his eyes glowing blue-green. "You'd better be glad about that. I'm seeing just as many water glyphs here as I did in Greta's room back at Brookhaven."

Kaz's forehead wrinkled up as Brett's and Lily's eyes returned to normal. "Air for your uncle, Gabe, and water for Greta?"

Gabe nodded. "Can't be a coincidence."

"Come on." Lily started for the door Jackson had disappeared through. "Let's explore this place."

3

The town house was enormous, clearly built and owned by people with a *lot* of money, but except for the kitchen and bathrooms, it was also incredibly old-fashioned. "Wow," Kaz said, wandering from the living room into the foyer. "Are we totally sure this is a house, and not, like, a museum?" Creaky wooden floors, hideously ugly wallpaper, and massive furniture dominated the decor.

Plus it smells like mothballs and feet.

"Hey, guys," Brett called out. "Come check out the dining room."

As he followed Kaz and Lily, Gabe asked, "What happened to Ghost Boy, anyway?"

As if in answer, they heard footsteps thumping overhead. Lily poked a thumb at the ceiling. "Second floor, I guess. Who knows what he's doing up there."

Gabe snorted. "He can stay up there for all I care."

They walked into the dining room, where Brett spread his arms out. "Take a look at all this!"

Gabe paused in the doorway and whistled softly through his teeth. The dining room had been converted into a . . . research center, he supposed would be accurate, but he wanted to call it a war room. Four free-standing whiteboards took up a lot of space along the walls, and the huge, heavy dining table was all but blanketed with papers, notebooks, and massive, ancient-looking books. *It's like Uncle Steve's office exploded in here.* Other than a single sleek laptop, the materials around the room were all pretty traditional.

Kaz picked up one of the papers. "We wanted research on Arcadia, right?" He waved the paper at Gabe. "Well, here it is. This is your uncle's handwriting, isn't it?"

Gabe took the paper. "Yeah." He picked up one of the notebooks. "This is different, though. Looks . . . neater, right? More legible and organized."

Lily peered over his shoulder. "I'll bet you ten bucks that's Greta's writing."

Brett picked up one of the two coffee mugs at the far end of the table and turned it upside down. "I think this brown crust in here used to be coffee." He set the cup back down. "If two people were going to get together and research how to destroy a magickal demon dimension, this looks like the place they'd do it."

One of the whiteboards caught Gabe's eye. He pointed. "Seriously. Look at that."

A symbol similar to a pentagram took up the center of the board, with four smaller symbols around its edge, color-coded: red, gray, blue, and green. *Fire, air, water, earth*. Eight or ten lines of text had been scrawled below the symbol, but—Gabe squinted—they were in Greek. No luck reading them.

However, inside the big five-pointed design, Gabe recognized the sun insignia from the robes the Eternal Dawn wore. And right beside it . . .

Kaz followed where Gabe was looking. "'Aria,'" Kaz read. The word hung in the air just as powerfully as a magickal glyph.

Gabe opened his mouth to speak, but his voice had caught in his throat. Instead, Brett spoke up. "Gabe's mom. I met her when I was in Arcadia."

Lily picked up one of the heavy books and started flipping through it. "Okay, so Dr. Conway and Greta got together here to figure out how to destroy Arcadia *and* rescue Gabe's mom. And that's exactly what we want to do. We should be able to find out what we need from their research, right?"

Lily's voice reached Gabe's ears as if from a great distance, rapidly replaced by a dull, pulsing roar. Gabe absently realized it was the pounding flow of his own blood. Fragments of thoughts tumbled over themselves in his mind.

Uncle Steve had been coming here, to this empty old house . . .

. . . with Greta Jaeger . . .

. . . for *who knows how many* years . . .

. . . to try to figure out how to rescue Gabe's mother.

It still shocked Gabe, how many and how huge were the secrets Uncle Steve had kept from him. Looking at the years of research around this dusty dining room, the revelations of the last few days hit him all at once. Gabe knew it wasn't, but the floor under his feet felt as if it were swaying back and forth. He put out a hand to steady himself, misjudged the distance, and almost fell past the table. A quick sidestep caught him.

How could he keep a whole life, a whole world *from me?*

No one seemed to have noticed Gabe's mini-meltdown, for which he felt enormously grateful. Answering Lily, Brett said, "Maybe. Except Dr. Conway and Greta didn't know you need five elements, instead of just four. That's why everything went so wrong the first time they tried to destroy Arcadia. They didn't know they needed magick to tie everything together."

The roaring filled Gabe's ears again. *Went so wrong . . .* that was an understatement if he'd ever heard one. The last time Uncle Steve, Greta, and Gabe's parents had tried to destroy Arcadia, Uncle Steve had lost his leg, Greta had gone insane, and both Gabe's parents had died.

Only it turned out that Gabe's mom *hadn't* died, and Uncle

Steve had suspected as much all along.

Brett's eyes shifted over to Gabe. "But now we know we need five elements. We might have to tweak some stuff to make it all work, but we *will* figure it out, Gabe. We'll get your mom and your uncle back. I promise."

Gabe gave Brett a weak smile. *I am so freaking lucky to have friends like these.* And before anyone could say anything else, Kaz's stomach rumbled so loudly it practically echoed around the room. Gabe chuckled. Meals had been hard to come by down in the tunnels. "So, who wants to see if the kitchen's stocked?"

As it turned out, the kitchen was stocked very well. Gabe could tell Uncle Steve had been the one buying the groceries because the cabinets and the fridge were full of his favorites. This made sense, given that Uncle Steve wasn't the one who was a fugitive from a mental institution. After a quick debate over the proper meal, in which both spaghetti and bacon and eggs were ruled out, Gabe slapped four thick hamburger patties onto a stove top grill.

He'd cook another one if Jackson ever showed up again. They could still hear Ghost Boy clomping around on the second floor. He'd ignored them both times they'd tried to call him down for dinner. Gabe knew it'd be a waste of time to go chasing after him. Jackson always did his own thing, and Gabe knew he would come down when he was good and ready and not a moment before.

Sitting at a small breakfast table in the kitchen, they all tore into their burgers with great gusto, but halfway through his, Kaz paused and dug into his pocket. Gabe swallowed the bite he'd been working on and wiped his mouth on a paper napkin. "What's up, Kaz?"

Kaz pulled out his phone, which was still buzzing. "It's my dad. He's texting me. Again."

Gabe kept his voice level. "Kaz . . . you know you can't respond to him, right? That was the whole point of hiding out in the tunnels. So nobody could track us. The last thing we want is the Eternal Dawn showing up at anybody's front door."

"No, I know. I'd never forgive myself if anything happened to my parents or my sisters. But Dad's getting really upset. Now he says if I don't text him back he's calling the cops."

When they first went underground, Kaz told his parents he was going on a sleepover. That had turned into a spur-of-the-moment camping trip, and after that he'd stopped responding altogether.

He stared down at the phone. "Dad's been leaving voice mails and sending emails . . . and so have Mom and all of my sisters. They're kind of . . ."

"Freaking out?" Lily put a comforting hand on his arm.

Kaz nodded.

Brett and Lily's parents were out of town and had left them to stay with their grandmother, who was a very nice old lady. A very nice, *gullible* old lady. She'd believed everything they'd told her about going on a white-water rafting trip with Kaz and the rest of the Smith family.

Gabe's only relatives were either dead or trapped in another dimension.

Kaz, on the other hand, had a huge, loving, worried-sick family not three miles from where they sat.

The phone buzzed in Kaz's hand. "Oh . . . crap." Kaz's face paled as his eyes flicked across the screen, and he held it up so everyone could see it.

To whomever is holding my son. It's not too late to release him. If you do so right now, there is a good chance you can escape before the police find you.

Kaz shoved his chair back from the table and started pacing, waving his hands as he stomped around the kitchen. "I can't put them through this! Dad'll have a heart attack. I mean, he probably won't, he's in great shape actually—he runs marathons—but what if my abduction traumatizes my sisters? What if they get PTSD and can't leave the house? They'll never get into college if they can't leave the house!"

Gabe leaned across the table toward Brett and Lily. "We

can't put him through this. Them either. He's got to check in with his family."

Lily nodded in agreement, but Brett made a sharp gesture with one hand. "It's too risky. What if he accidentally gives something away?"

Pain creased Lily's face. "But what if this is the only way to convince the Smiths that Kaz is all right?" She turned to Gabe. "What do you think?"

Kaz didn't give Gabe a chance to answer. He slapped a hand down on the table and said, "Guys, I'm sorry, but I'm calling. I've got no choice. I should've done this days ago."

Brett shifted in his seat, as if he might try to get up and stop Kaz, but Gabe grabbed his shoulder. "Brett, he's right. He's got no choice." Brett frowned, but he folded his arms across his chest, sank back into his seat, and stayed quiet.

Kaz tapped the screen. Gabe could hear the faint ringing, and the even fainter sound of Mr. Smith's voice. Kaz tried for a cheerful tone: "Hi, Dad!"

Gabe heard a burst of sound from the phone, and figured it was an explosion of words on the other end of the line. With each of Kaz's responses, his happy tone deteriorated further into shame and guilt.

"What? No, no, I'm fine! I'm with Gabe and Lily and Brett!"

"I know, I know, I'm sorry I've been out of touch, I . . ."

"No, look, Dad, everything's totally fine, it's . . ."

"*Huh?* You already called them? Dad, there's no reason to bring the cops into this! I'm telling you, I'm—"

Lily sprang from her chair, grabbed the phone out of Kaz's hand—"Hey!"—and stabbed the End button. She turned the phone off, took a couple of steps toward the kitchen island, and then began to riffle through one of its drawers.

"Lily, what are you—" Gabe asked.

He watched as, a moment later, she found a paper clip and went to work on the back of the phone. A second later she pulled out the phone's SIM card.

Wow—she thinks fast!

The whole time, Kaz stood staring at her, goggle-eyed. "Lily! What the *heck*? That's my *phone*! You can't just—"

"Sorry, Kaz, but if your dad already called the police, they were totally tracing that call."

Kaz sputtered. "But we turned off the GPS!"

Lily shook her head. "Doesn't matter. The cops can figure out which cell towers your call pinged off. I saw that on *CSI*."

"Great." Brett leaned back in his chair and laced his fingers behind his head. "So now what? We can't leave the house because the cops will be combing the streets for us?"

Lily glanced at Gabe while Kaz pouted. "What do we do?"

Gabe stood. He circled around and put his hands on the back of his chair. "We need to get rid of all our SIM cards." He grabbed the paper clip and popped his own phone's card loose. "Come on. Everybody." He waited while Lily and Brett did the same. "Give them to me, okay? I'll make sure they're trashed." Once he had all four SIM cards in his hand, he said, "Look . . . I don't think there's anything we can do about the cops right now. But we've got all of Uncle Steve's and Greta's research right here, don't we? We've got full stomachs, we're protected by a billion air and water wards . . . let's just lie low, put this time to good use, and try to figure something out."

If Kaz had had more hair, his eyebrows would have been in danger of disappearing into it. "How do you know the wards will protect us? They didn't make any difference at your house."

"Do not worry." Jackson Wright came strolling into the kitchen and leaned against the counter, as if he hadn't just disappeared for forty-five minutes. "Few things can penetrate the walls of this house."

"Oh yeah?" Gabe turned to face him, not bothering to hide his suspicion. "And how exactly do you know that?"

"These walls are lined with thrice-warded Egyptian silver, Gabriel. I watched them lay it in myself over a century ago, though I knew not at the time what I was witnessing." Jackson gestured grandly about him. "This is Argent Court. This is my home."

Gabe's jaw dropped. "You used to *live* here?"

Jackson's normally sour expression grew even more acerbic. He held out a photograph to Gabe—a faded Polaroid of Gabe's mother and father holding an infant, all three of them posing on the front steps of an old-fashioned house.

This house!

Even after a week of incredible shocks, Gabe still reeled at the sight.

Everything he knew about his life, or believed he knew, seemed as baffling and unfamiliar as if it had belonged to a complete stranger.

"I did indeed live here, Gabriel," Jackson sniffed. "And a century later, it appears, so did you."

4

L ily woke to deep confusion, staring up at the tin ceiling of the dusty bedroom. *What was that sound?* A glance at the window showed her that it was still dark. She flipped on the nightstand lamp, and a bleary peek at an old-fashioned alarm clock confirmed the hour: 2:37 a.m.

Between her exhausted slumber and the unfamiliar surroundings, it took her a good ten seconds after she opened her eyes to remember where she was. She sat up and swung her legs over the edge of the bed, running one hand through her short, tousled hair. Despite her bleariness, she couldn't help grinning as her eyes fell on the door of the en suite bath.

After twelve years of sharing a bathroom with her brother,

having one all to herself felt like some kind of royal luxury.

She pulled on the thick terry-cloth robe she'd found hanging in the bathroom. She had one hand on the door to the hallway when she heard faint voices. *That must be what woke me up.* Lily opened the door and poked her head out, listening. She was the only one on this level, since Brett, Gabe, and Kaz had rushed all the way up to the fourth floor to find places to sleep. Lily was happy enough not to climb more stairs. The second-floor bedroom she'd found was perfect. Jackson had announced that, should anyone need to find him, he'd be in his old room on the third floor.

Watching the former Ghost Boy trudge up the stairs, Lily had felt kind of sorry for him. Yes, he was the one whose lies had gotten both Dr. Conway and Brett sent to Arcadia, where Brett could have been killed and . . . Dr. Conway still might be. She still wanted to clock Jackson in his pasty face for that one. For the thousandth time, she said a quick prayer for the safety of Gabe's uncle. But if she tried to put herself in Jackson's shoes . . . she really couldn't imagine how she'd feel. Coming back to a world a century ahead of the one she'd left behind? All her family and friends long dead? *What a nightmare.*

She couldn't tell exactly how Jackson felt about it. Lily wasn't even sure Jackson was glad to be back on this plane of existence, since he acted so miserable all the time.

She heard the voices again, echoing up the stairwell from below, one male, one female. The male voice sounded like

Brett, but who could the woman be? *Oh no—did the cops find us?* Heart racing, Lily tiptoed down the hall and descended the ornate stairway, careful to not make any noise.

An unexpected scent reached her nose when she got to the ground floor. She knew it well, as did anyone who'd spent any time in San Francisco: an ocean breeze. In this stuffy, sealed-up house, it struck her as immensely strange, and as she crept toward the dining room—the source of the voices—her skin prickled with gooseflesh. *Feels like a storm's coming.* Dim, flickering yellow light emanated from the room, casting dancing shadows on the wall of the hallway outside the door.

Lily peeked into the room, but it was hard to make sense of the shapes and silhouettes of the dimly lit space, and before she even really thought about it, her hand whipped out and flicked on the electric light switch. The chandelier over the dining table popped to life, flooding the room with bright-white light, and the before-the-storm feeling abruptly vanished.

Her brother sat at the table across from an unfamiliar woman with long, straight, blue-black hair and skin pale as milk. Until Lily turned on the overhead lights, the room had been lit only by a dozen candles. And maybe the candles cast strange shadows, illuminating things in unexpected ways—because for a heartbeat, Brett's face didn't look like . . . like *his face.*

Lily sucked in a sharp breath and took a step back.

Brett grinned, his face back to normal. Had it been anything *but* normal? *Was I seeing things?* Brett said, *"Hola, hermana."*

Heart hammering against her ribs, Lily hovered in the dining room doorway. "What are you doing? Who's this?"

The pale woman watched Lily with wide, placid blue eyes and said nothing.

Brett spread his hands on the table. "I couldn't sleep, so I figured I'd try to do something useful."

Lily took a step into the room. The pale woman tracked her movements, her expression unchanging. Lily cleared her throat. "Who are you?"

From behind Lily, Gabe's voice rang out. *"Mom?"*

Lily turned and saw Gabe standing there in his boxer shorts, looking as if someone had just struck him between the eyes with a two-by-four. Emotions chased themselves across his face: confusion, hope, fear, love. Tears welled up in his eyes, and he dashed into the room and threw his arms around the woman. *"Mom!"*

Horror settled around Lily like a bank of freezing mist as the pale woman's skin rippled and flowed at Gabe's touch. Then all Lily could hear was the sound of Gabe screaming.

Lily, Kaz, Jackson, and Brett sat around the dining table, and the thing that looked like Aria, Gabe's mother, remained in its place. Only Gabe was standing. He was back in the corner of the room the farthest away from the pale female shape, his eyes still red and puffy from the sudden burst of tears. He'd furiously wiped his cheeks dry.

Cheeks exactly the same color as the woman's skin. Lily's eyes flicked back and forth from Gabe to the thing in the chair.

"Why does this *thing*—this apographon—look like my mom?" The tremors had finally left his voice. Lily had never seen Gabe this freaked out before. Not that she could blame him. "Brett, did you . . . did you do this?" His volume increased as he stared at the pale figure. *"What are you?"*

"My name is Aria," the figure said, in a tone all the more horrifying because it sounded so dead and wooden.

Gabe snorted and folded his arms across his chest.

Lily pursed her lips as a deep pang of sympathy shot through her. *What would I have done if this thing had looked like Charlie?* The memory of her older brother loomed large.

Brett sighed. "Look, there's a reason I did this, okay? Just, just try to follow me here." He held up a thin stack of pages, covered in Greta's graceful, looping handwriting, and waved it at the group. "Dr. Conway and Greta always believed Aria might have survived that last ritual. The one where they tried to destroy Arcadia, that ended up being a disaster."

Lily stared at the tabletop. That was the very same ritual they were currently working so hard to re-create.

Brett went on. "Dr. Conway and Greta were air and water. They thought they needed fire and earth—they didn't know they needed magick."

Lily could see Jackson's jaw tighten, but he didn't say anything.

"They also knew how dangerous working this kind of magick can get, so they didn't want to bring in any new people if they could help it. That's why they decided to see if they could get Gabe's mom to help them. *From* Arcadia." Brett held up a small book bound in red leather. Lily couldn't work out the title, what with Brett waving it around, but the words appeared to be French. "I found this under a pile of diary pages. It's called *Whisper of the Remains*, more or less."

Lily raised an eyebrow. "You speak French? Since when?"

Brett grinned. "Well, there was this girl I liked, and she was taking a French class. She had really curly hair and . . ." Lily rolled her eyes and sighed. "Right, not relevant, sorry. Anyway, according to this"—he tapped the red book—"an apographon is able to mimic a person by synching with his or her consciousness. This one was created to look like Gabe's mom because they were trying to make a connection to her in Arcadia. They figured that they could maybe talk with her through it and get her to help them pull off another ritual."

"Wait. Hang on," Kaz said. "If this is the apographon from Greta's room, then how come it's sitting up and talking now? It was just a pile of disguised rocks and wood back when it looked like Greta."

"That's the thing," Brett said. "While Greta was alive, the

apographon was a perfect copy. It could probably talk like her and answer questions and everything. But since she died—once the consciousness it was linked to went quiet—it went . . . inert, I guess. Dr. Conway and Greta ran into a similar problem when trying to connect with Gabe's mom. This thing might look and sound like her, but, as you can see, you don't have to be a rocket scientist to know there's something really *not right* about her."

Lily frowned. "Because Arcadia was too far away for it to make a good connection?"

"Exactly," Brett said. "So when connecting to Gabe's mom failed, I'm guessing Greta must have reprogrammed it to look like herself and used it to cover for her when she slipped out of Brookhaven." Brett looked over at Gabe, sort of apologetically. "I was checking the apographon out, and I found this . . . sort of a residue. Like, just a trace of your mom. I didn't mean to freak you out, but this is good news, right? The fact that it's moving and talking at all proves that your mom is still alive in Arcadia. I know it's not the real thing, but—"

Gabe pushed off from the wall and tore his eyes away from the apographon. He drifted out of the room, his face so haunted Lily thought he looked more like a ghost than Jackson ever had. As he passed through the doorway, over his shoulder he said, "Get rid of it. I don't want to see it anymore."

Brett half stood. "But Gabe! Wait! We need it! Studying this thing could help us!"

Gabe paused, his back to them. "I don't care. I want it gone."

As Gabe disappeared down the hallway, Lily couldn't help wondering how terrible it had to feel, finding something that looked so much like the person you'd lost, only to find out that it was a lie.

5

Gabe sat between his mother and father as they cruised down the country road in his father's pickup. They were on their way to the movies, and his taste buds were all set for heavily buttered popcorn. He watched the way his father's hands gripped the wheel, the lines of muscle in his father's forearms. Gabe hoped he'd be as strong as his dad one day.

"Excited, honey?" his mother asked, and twined her fingers through Gabe's. Her skin was smooth and cool, and he nestled against her, the heavy curtain of her long black hair falling around him.

"I can't wait! It's supposed to be awesome!"

His mother patted his hair and rested the side of her face against the top of his head.

"I'm afraid we're going to be late, son," Gabe's father said, and let his foot sink farther toward the floorboard. The pickup's engine growled as they accelerated. The trees along the side of the road became greenish-brown blurs.

"Now, now, sweetheart, we've got plenty of time." Gabe's mother put a finger under Gabe's chin and tipped his face up to look at her.

Gabe glanced at his dad behind the wheel and saw that his eyes were on fire. Twin suns that could burn through anything. The fire spread across his father's face, and searing pain lanced through Gabe's hands, because they were on fire, too.

His mother leaned forward and whispered in his ear, *"We will always be a family."*

Gabe turned toward his father and screamed.

The driver's seat was an inferno.

Arms made of flame encircled Gabe as the pickup veered off the road, and he tried to reach the door, tried to jump out, but he couldn't. The flames held him tightly as they seared through his clothes and his flesh and his bones, and the truck hurtled down a rocky cliff face, and Gabe knew he would die in a massive ball of fire. . . .

And in his head a rough, whispered voice chanted, *Burn . . . burn . . . burn . . .*

Gabe's eyes sprang open. His badly trembling hand switched on the light beside his bed, and he stared around at the Argent Court bedroom, convincing himself, *willing* himself to believe that *this* was real, *this* was reality.

Not that dream.

That nightmare.

He swung his legs over the edge of the bed and sat there with his knees on his elbows, staring at the floor. His toes dug into the nap of the rug covering the hardwood. His fingertips gingerly checked for burns, and when they found none, he finally breathed an unsteady sigh of relief. There was no fire. *There was no fire.*

Weak early-morning light the color of dirty dishwater leaked in around the heavy curtains. Gabe didn't know if he *could* go back to sleep, but he was a hundred percent certain he didn't *want* to. Moving slowly, he stood and pulled on his clothes again.

Details of his encounter with the Mom-shaped apographon came back to him bit by bit, whether he wanted them to or not. *No wonder I had nightmares.* Gabe decided to concentrate on breakfast, or at least try to. He trudged down the stairs.

The lights in the dining room were still on, so Gabe stopped there before he even reached the kitchen. Brett was still sitting in the same chair, like he was glued to it, with the Emerald Tablet and one of Uncle Steve's notebooks open in front of him.

"Morning," Gabe said. He didn't know what to think about

this new, studious Brett Hernandez. The most he'd ever known Brett to read before was video game item descriptions, but since he'd come back from Arcadia, Brett had taken to books like a cat to catnip. Of all the ways Brett could be coping with the experience, Gabe figured this had to be one of the better ones. It was just weird, was all.

Brett didn't look up, and the grunt he made didn't even count as a word. But Gabe nearly jumped when, from the shadows in one corner, Jackson Wright said, "You look as if you haven't slept in a year."

Gabe composed himself. Barely. "Could you *try* not being weird and creepy? Just once? Or is that too much for you?"

Jackson, standing there with his arms folded, went back to watching Brett, which it seemed he'd been doing for a while. Gabe couldn't tell if Brett had even gone to bed at all. "Yes, Gabriel, I'm *so* inspired to be pleasant to you," Jackson said. "Because of your open, honest, forgiving nature."

Gabe fell silent and headed toward the kitchen again. Weird and creepy Jackson might be, but Gabe *had* tried to shove him into a shadow dimension. Shame made him feel heavier.

Someone had already made a pot of . . . Gabe sniffed. *Is that tea?* It looked a little weak. And what appeared to be a fresh tin of muffins sat on the stove top, untouched. Gabe poured a mug and ignored the muffins. He wandered out into the living room—one of the more opulently decorated rooms in an already opulently decorated house, with huge, heavy, mahogany furniture upholstered in burgundy silk—and found Kaz curled up on one of the couches. His knees were pulled up to his chest, and his hoodie stretched all the way down over his legs, which made him look like a blue M&M.

Gabe noticed the laptop they'd found in the dining room open on the coffee table.

"You got into it?" he asked, pointing to the computer. They'd been so busy the night before with all the books and notes Uncle Steve and Greta had left behind, they hadn't even gotten to the laptop.

"Yeah, it had the same password as the one in his home office," Kaz said. "You know, your, uh, birthday." Thinking again of how crappy he'd been to Uncle Steve the last time they spoke, Gabe felt a spike of regret in his gut. Kaz must have seen the look on Gabe's face because he quickly continued. "Anyway—there's not much on here. Looks like he mostly used it for his university email."

"I guess that makes sense," Gabe said. "He was an old-school kind of guy. Would rather trek all the way across town to some moldy library than google something." Gabe blinked and wiped the back of his hand over his eyes to stop the tears. Being around his uncle's things made him miss him even more—but he had to focus.

"But check this out." Kaz nudged the laptop over to Gabe.

Gabe picked up the computer and sucked in a quick breath. It was a video embedded in a news report. The volume was down, but the video showed a swarm of demonic-looking abyssal bats clustering on the island. *There are thousands of them! Maybe more!*

The headline across the top of the screen read, "Mysterious Mass Migration of North American Condors."

"It's the breach to Arcadia we accidentally opened during the last ritual," Kaz said darkly. "The Dawn must be using the power coming through it to create an army."

The mass of bats surrounding the prison isle was easily a hundred times the size of the force they'd fought on Alcatraz three days ago. "We have to stop them," Gabe said.

"But how? There are already a million abyssal bats, and think of what just one of them did to—to—" Kaz didn't finish the sentence because he didn't have to. Gabe knew he was talking about Greta.

"First we have to figure out this ritual. Then we'll make our move," Gabe said. It sounded easy, but it wasn't. It was just about the furthest thing from easy he could think of. But one thing at a time. "Were you the one who made breakfast?"

Kaz stared forlornly at his own cup of tea. "The milk was about to go bad, so I made muffins. Or at least, I followed the directions on the box. They *look* like muffins. I tried to do some tea, too, like Mom makes it, but I don't think I got it right." He sighed. "It doesn't matter, I guess, since we don't have any maple syrup, either."

Whenever Gabe had gone with Kaz, Brett, and Lily on one

of their urban-exploration "field trips," Kaz always brought a thermos of tea for them to share. He always remembered that Gabe liked his sweetened with maple syrup. Gabe tried to remember the last time he'd had any. It had been less than a week ago, but it seemed like another lifetime.

Gabe sat down on the couch. Kaz just kept staring at his cup. It was still full.

Worrying about his family is eating him alive.

"Look, Kaz, you're doing the right thing." Gabe set his tea down on the floor. "Keeping your parents and sisters out of this? You're keeping them safe. You know that, right?"

Kaz touched his temple. "I know it up *here*." He thumped his chest. "It's just *here* that it sucks so hard. They really think I've been kidnapped! They're worried sick."

Gabe nodded. "I know. I *know*. But you don't want your family to end up like mine." Kaz pulled his eyes away from his mug to look at Gabe. Gabe went on. "Everybody in my family is either dead or trapped in Arcadia, and it's because of all this crazy elemental stuff we're wrapped up in. Your family's safe. And you will see them again. Dude, I promise you. You will."

Kaz tried a smile. It didn't look convincing.

Gabe stood up. "Have you eaten anything?" When Kaz shook his head, Gabe beckoned. "Come on, at least have a muffin. I mean, you made them, you've gotta try one." After a moment, Kaz shrugged and stood. He trailed after Gabe to the kitchen, and Gabe found a tub of butter in the fridge, which he smeared on a muffin like it was frosting.

Kaz eyed the pastry warily. "Jeez, Gabe, are you trying to give me a heart attack with all that butter? How am I supposed to be a, like, a good earth elementalist if I'm always grabbing my chest and keeling over?" But he picked up the muffin and took a big bite anyway, and the earlier trace of a smile came back, this time with a little more strength.

Lily wandered in, rubbing her eyes. She was back in her regular clothes, which were rumpled but looked a lot cleaner than Gabe's. "Morning. What's going on? Did I miss any more insanity?"

Around a mouthful, Kaz said, "Nah. Gabe was just nicing at me."

Lily sat down across from Gabe and smirked. "Nicing? Is that a word?"

Kaz swallowed, nodding. "Trying to make me feel better." He took a sip of tea. "When we should be nicing at him instead."

Huh?

But Lily seemed to get what Kaz was talking about. She turned her dark eyes to Gabe. "Gabe, you know it's really important to stay positive while we're going through all of this. We have to believe it's going to come out all right. But if it doesn't . . ."

Before Gabe could figure out where this was going, Kaz

said, "Just, you should know, man. We've got your back. I mean, Mom and Dad already have a bunch of kids. What's one more?"

Lily said, "Or, I mean, you'd be totally welcome at our place. You could . . ." She paused. "You could take Charlie's old room. It'd be good for somebody to sleep in there again."

Gabe sat back in his chair. It took a few seconds for his mouth to make sounds again. *They're trying to take care of me in case I don't see any of my family again. In case Uncle Steve and my mom . . . don't make it back.* "Have you two talked about this before? You have, haven't you?"

Kaz and Lily exchanged guilty glances. Lily said, "We just want you to know you've got somebody. You're not going to end up by yourself."

Gabe turned away from them so they wouldn't see the tears in his eyes. He'd already gone to pieces in front of them once, when he realized the apographon wasn't really his mother. He couldn't do it again.

Get a grip, Gabe! Everyone's counting on you!

"Thanks, guys," Gabe managed to squeak out. But these words didn't nearly begin to cover the gratitude he felt.

Kaz and Lily and Brett were his friends. *Real* friends.

No, Gabe realized.

They were more than friends. Even if he didn't see his uncle or his mother again . . . he knew he still had a family.

Full of watered-down tea and muffins, Gabe led Kaz and Lily into the dining room, where Brett still sat hunched over the Emerald Tablet and stacks of paper choked with handwriting. Ghost Boy still lurked in the corner, watching Brett like a hawk. The apographon lay in another corner, back to its stone-golem appearance. Fighting off a shiver of disgust, Gabe pulled back the chair it had occupied and sat down across from Brett. "You're starting to look like some kind of mad scientist, dude."

Brett grunted. "From what I can tell, Greta and your uncle almost had everything worked out. It won't take all that much to recalibrate the ritual so it uses all five elements. And maybe—if we're smart about it—we can figure out how to get Dr. Conway and your mom back before we destroy Arcadia, too."

Gabe surprised himself by grinning. "That's great!" *We finally have a clue as to what to do next!*

Kaz was just as excited. "Really? Like how? What do we need to do?" He circled the table to look over Brett's shoulder, and Brett rattled off a flurry of what might as well have been Klingon to Gabe. He understood the individual words, but the way Brett had put them together, it was just a wall of information. Gabe had never been a star student even when he was studying normal things like history or biology, and he was *totally* out of his depth with this stuff. He was just glad it seemed to make sense to Kaz and Brett.

"I've gotta say, Brett, I never thought you would get all

into research like this," Gabe said.

Brett broke off talking to Kaz to spear Jackson with a pointed look. "Yeah, well, there's nothing like getting trapped in a magickal nightmare world to make you reexamine your priorities."

Gabe shrugged. *Can't argue with that.*

Then a dark thought made his eyebrows draw together. *What if we can't do both? What if we can't get Mom and Uncle Steve back* and *destroy Arcadia?* He shuddered. *What if we have to choose?*

"It comes down to a reagent, I think," Brett said. As if to answer Gabe's unspoken question, he held up a ring. "A reagent is an ingredient for a spell. In this case, this ring."

Jackson gasped at the sight of it.

Gabe squinted at it. *That's a signet ring—the kind of thing they used to mash into hot wax to seal letters with.* It had a pretty simple design, a circle with five lines radiating from the center.

Kaz took the ring from Brett, and Lily came over to get a look at it. "What's the big deal about it?" Kaz asked.

Jackson rasped out, "I shall *tell* you what the 'big deal' is. It bears my family crest—'Wright' was shortened from 'Wheelwright' in the early eighteenth century—but the ring's origins far predate my family's."

Gabe looked at the design of the ring again. He guessed it did sort of look like a wheel. But wouldn't a wagon wheel have more than five spokes?

"That ring, according to lore, was fashioned from metal found in a meteorite," Jackson went on. "It cannot—"

Brett cut Jackson off with a wave of his hand. "Yes, yes, it's very old, we get it. Don't worry, Ghost Boy, I won't hurt your precious family heirloom."

Jackson glowered at Brett with enough force to peel paint. "Pardon me, but my concern is not for the ring, but for *us*— indeed, for our entire world. As much occult knowledge as the Eternal Dawn, or Steven Conway and Greta Jaeger, have collected, a thousand times that has been lost over the course of millennia. You cannot begin to know the effect that using the ring may—"

"Listen, I'm trying to *do something*," Brett snarled. "Researching, reading, calculating. And what are you doing? The same thing you've been doing for the last hundred years: absolutely *nothing*. You whine, you sulk, you lash out, and that's it. Because that's all you're good for: getting in everyone else's way."

Even Jackson seemed taken aback by Brett's venom.

I'm not exactly a fan of Jackson's, but Brett sounds like he straight-up hates the guy.

Everyone at the table jumped when the doorbell rang. Gabe turned to Jackson. "Who's *that*? No one knows we're here. Is it the cops?"

Jackson threw his hands up. "Why are you asking *me*? Am I standing at the front door? Honestly, Gabriel."

Kaz jammed the ring into his hoodie's big front pocket and frantically started sorting and collecting the piles of paper on the table. Brett clamped a hand down on Kaz's wrist. "What do you think you're doing?"

"We've got to hide all this stuff and get out of here!" Kaz's voice rose in pitch. "What if the bad guys found us?" He pointed at the apographon. "Somebody needs to throw a sheet over Rocky there, too!"

Jackson scowled at them all. "One thing I *will* say. No one should have been able to trace us here. The way this house is warded? The silver in the walls? We are standing in a fortress."

"Okay, everyone calm down," Gabe said. "Let me go see who it is, and I'll try to get rid of them." No one objected to that, so Gabe crossed through the foyer to the front door, peered through the curtains of the small window set into it, and felt his stomach fall right into his shoes. He turned to see everyone else watching him from the dining room door, and he mouthed the words: *It's the cops!*

Kaz gasped, before Lily put a hand over his mouth.

Gabe understood how they felt. The last time police had shown up at his door, they'd turned out to be agents of the Eternal Dawn, and sicced a pair of hunters—eyeless, skinless horrors the size of small ponies—on them. Gabe had practically had to burn his own house down so he and his friends could get away.

Gabe thought as fast as he could. This was bad, even if

these were regular, run-of-the-mill cops, considering they were a group of unaccompanied minors with at least one official missing person among them. He turned on his brightest smile as he opened the door. He took a deep breath. "Can I help you, Officers?"

Both cops were black, one a short, chunky man, the other a tall, thin woman. Their name tags proclaimed the man to be Officer Cook, and the woman to be Officer Dante. "Hey there, son," Officer Cook said. "Are your parents home?"

"Not right now, no," Gabe said, relieved and amazed that he hadn't stuttered. "I mean, I live with my uncle."

Officer Cook held out a phone with a photo of Kaz on it. "Well, we're looking for a missing boy, about your age, and we traced his cell signal to this neighborhood. Have you seen this kid?"

Ugh, Lily was right about the cell signal!

Gabe scrunched up his face. "He looks familiar . . . I might have seen him around, I just can't place where."

Officer Dante tried to look into the house over Gabe's shoulder. "May we speak to your uncle?"

Be convincing! "Like I said, he's not here right now. Could you maybe try back later?"

Officer Cook seemed impatient, like he'd rather be done with this and move on to the next house, but Officer Dante got a look on her face that Gabe recognized. It was the same look Uncle Steve got when he could tell Gabe was lying about something. "What's your name, young man? And your uncle's name?"

Gabe wasn't sure whether it came from his nerves, or his quick thinking, or maybe quick thinking fueled by nerves, but he sent a burst of fire energy into the street and thought, *Now!*

A manhole cover exploded up out of the pavement, billowed aloft on a cloud of hissing steam, and bounced off the side of the patrol car parked in front of the house. Both Cook and Dante yelped and scrambled off the porch, barking into their radios.

Gabe slammed the door and put his back against it while everyone else rushed forward. "Okay, I just bought us a little time, I think, but that lady cop is totally onto me. What do we do?"

"There is room for them in the basement," Jackson said speculatively, before everyone else stared him down. "What? Do you have a better notion?"

"We're not kidnapping innocent cops and putting them in the basement!" Gabe barked.

"You're sure they're innocent?" Lily peered out the little window.

"Pretty sure. I didn't get any Dawn-ish vibes from them while we were talking."

"Well, we can't send Kaz with them, no matter what." Brett chucked Kaz on the shoulder. "We need you to stop the apocalypse, buddy."

Kaz didn't rise to Brett's casual remark, and he looked gloomier than usual when he said, "If I did go back home now, Dad wouldn't let me out of my room until I was forty."

"Wait a minute!" Lily said excitedly. "The, the *thing*, we can use the rock thing!" She pointed to the golem that lay collapsed in the corner. "The apographon! Send it with the cops!"

"Yes!" Gabe nodded furiously. "We can make it look like Kaz! Lily, you're a genius! Brett, do you think you could pull that off?"

A smile slowly spread across Brett's lips. "Of course I can!"

"It's not that easy, you fool," Jackson snorted. "Reverting the apographon to its previous appearance of Gabriel's mother was one thing. But creating a link between it and Kazuo's consciousness is utterly beyond your abilities."

"Thanks, Ghost Boy," Brett said, gathering the apographon's strange humanlike form up from the floor. "Forget the cops—now I'll do it just to prove you wrong."

They heard footfalls coming up the front steps.

"Well, you'd better do it really freaking fast, then," Kaz said.

Once everyone else had scurried back into the dining room, Gabe waited until the cops had knocked on the door twice before he opened it again. "Oh, hi, Officers. Did you forget something?"

Officer Cook, who had looked bored, now looked bored

and annoyed, and Gabe decided he'd better tone down the smart-aleck before Cook decided to take that annoyance out on him. Officer Dante's suspicious expression had only deepened. Gabe noticed the manhole cover was back in place.

"We forgot to get your name and your uncle's name," Dante said with a tight jaw.

"Oh! Oh, right. My name is Gabe."

Never taking her eyes off him, Dante pulled out a notepad and jotted that down. "Last name?"

"Excuse me?"

"Your last name. What is it?"

Stall, stall, come on, Gabe!

"*My* last name? Don't you want my uncle's name?"

Dante sighed. "Yes, we want your uncle's name, too."

"Oh, his name is Steve."

Dante's eyes narrowed, and Officer Cook made a growling sound in his throat. *Hurry up, guys!* "Hey, y'know, I was thinking, I might've remembered where I saw that kid on your phone before."

Dante dropped her hands to her sides. "Yeah? *Where?*"

"Well, I've got some friends over, playing video games, y'know, because that's what us young people do, and that kid might be a friend of a friend. So he might actually be here after all?"

Officer Cook put his hand on the doorknob. Gabe had

no illusions about his ability to keep hold of the door if Cook decided to push it the rest of the way open. "You're saying Kazuo Smith is here now? Where?"

Keeeeeep stalllllliiiiing!

"Well, he might be in the bathroom, come to think of it . . . we were eating some hot wings, so you might want to give him a minute or two. . . ."

Officer Dante's voice went from chilly to arctic. "Where is this bathroom, *exactly?*"

Gabe's mind raced—*What do I say? I can't act any dumber than I already have been*—but before he could say a word, he felt a wave of power rush through him, emanating from back inside the house. *The apographon, I hope!* Neither Dante nor Cook seemed to notice anything, though, which made Gabe feel even more sure they weren't connected to the Eternal Dawn.

"Hey! I just got here. Are these nice policepersons looking for me?"

Gabe looked over his shoulder, and for a second almost panicked, because it was Kaz strolling up to the door from the dining room, tugging on his hoodie. Or was it?

Cook did push the door open at that point. "Kazuo Smith?"

"That's me!" Kaz said, and winked at Gabe surreptitiously. "Wait, did my father send you guys after me? I *told* him I was fine!"

Officer Dante shoved her notepad and pen back into her pocket and took Kaz by the arm. "You're coming with us, young man." She stabbed a glare at Gabe. "And then Officer Cook and I are going to come back and have a word with you. *And* your uncle."

"See ya!" Kaz chirped to Gabe as the cops led him down the steps. Gabe watched until the patrol car had driven away before he sprinted back to the dining room.

The real Kaz stood there, grinning ear-to-ear. "Who says you can't be in two places at once?"

Gabe stared at Kaz. "That was . . . I . . . wow. *Wow.* That thing was *convincing.*"

Brett nodded. "That's how it's *supposed* to work. When the person it's copying isn't dead or trapped in another dimension."

Kaz half-leaned, half-sat against the table. "I feel totally wiped out all of a sudden."

"I think that's normal." Brett peered into Kaz's eyes like a doctor. "You should feel some fatigue, but your mind will still be sharp." He chucked Kaz on the shoulder again. "Well. As sharp as it usually is, anyway." Kaz stuck his tongue out at Brett.

Jackson moved around to the other side of the table and curled his mouth as if he smelled something unpleasant. "Well, that was a very neat trick. Exactly how, Mr. Hernandez, did you activate the apographon so quickly and skillfully?"

Brett's teasing grin vanished. "How? By *studying.* Instead of standing around sulking all the time."

"Someone who has had all of three days to *study* spellwork

should not have been able to accomplish what you did. Explain yourself," Jackson demanded.

"I bet it's tough finding out that you're not as smart as you thought, isn't it, Ghost Boy?" Brett laughed. "Well, get over it. And get used to it."

Jackson folded his arms. "And now that I ponder it, how did those constables come to find us here? The protections of this house being what they are? Someone not possessed of any Art should not even have been able to *see* this place."

Lily stepped close to her brother. Gabe had seen the Hernandez twins do that countless times—if anything threatened either of them, no matter what it was, they closed ranks. Lily said, "Jackson, give it a rest. Yeah, it's got magickal protection, but that doesn't have any effect on cell phone signals. There are cell towers all over San Francisco, and Nob Hill is no exception. It's probably a miracle they didn't trace Kaz's phone faster."

Jackson sneered. "Or perhaps *someone* damaged the wards with his reckless tinkering with powers he couldn't possibly understand!"

"Sounds like you're the one having trouble *understanding*," Brett said, raising his voice. "You think you know a thing about cell phones when you hadn't even seen a lightbulb until three days ago? How's the data coverage in the Umbra, anyway?" Brett glanced at Gabe. "Help me out here, will you?"

"He's right, Jackson," Gabe said. "Technology and magick are different things. Just because the cops can trace a cell phone doesn't mean the Dawn will be able to find us."

But Jackson didn't back down. He folded his arms. "I demand that we check the wards again."

Brett rolled his eyes and looked like he was about to launch into Jackson all over again, when Lily stopped him with a hand on his shoulder.

"Let's just do it, *hermano*. It's easier."

"Fine." Brett sighed. "Do what you have to do."

With a boost of magick from Jackson, Lily and Brett lit up the protective wards again so Gabe and Kaz could see them, too. Gabe didn't *think* anything was out of place, but as they moved through the house, he had to admit to himself that he wouldn't have been able to tell if it was. The wards were inscribed in the glyphs of water and air, and Gabe couldn't make sense of any of them.

"Satisfied?" Brett finally asked when they stopped in the foyer.

Jackson's eyes transitioned from gold back to their normal icy blue. "Not remotely."

A thorny silence descended. If either Jackson or Brett's elements had been fire, Gabe was pretty sure the stares they fixed on each other would have set both of them ablaze. Gabe tried to think of something, anything, to say that might break the tension and get them all back on track. Fighting among themselves wasn't going to get them anywhere.

But before Gabe could speak, a pale tentacle as thick as a tree trunk smashed through a streetside window and splattered golden slime everywhere as it reached for him.

6

Gabe stood rooted to the floor as the tentacle drilled through the air toward him, and everything in his stomach turned to ice water. It seemed as if the tentacle was moving in slow motion, and every ripple of its slime-coated muscles stood out in excruciating detail.

Gabe recognized it. *It's like the thing on the ceiling in Greta's hospital room!* Except this one was bigger. *So much* bigger.

Time returned to normal between one heartbeat and the next, and Gabe grabbed the two people nearest him, Kaz and Lily, and hauled them out of the way just as the silvery glyphs around the window sprang to life and detonated with a sound like a clap of thunder. The tentacle dropped to the parquet floor, severed, and after a few violent flops finally came to rest.

Before Gabe could even take a breath, the house shook so violently all five of them lurched and stumbled, and another tentacle shot through the already-shattered window. Nothing slowed this one down. *Those glyphs were like the ones at my house! Single-use!* "Get back!" Gabe screamed. "Get away from it!" The house shuddered again, and the air filled with the sound of breaking glass, followed immediately by more crashing explosions.

Another tentacle clawed toward them from a parlor window, gliding over a severed one that now quivered on the floor. Gabe drew fire from the house's main power line, threw out his right hand, and hit the approaching tentacle with a column of flame so hot its center burned white. The tentacle spasmed as its tissue charred and crumbled away, and finally its owner pulled the blackened stump back out of the window.

Gabe whooped. "We can fight it! *We can fight it!*"

Then a familiar howling cut through the house, and Gabe felt his entire body become a goose bump.

Lily screamed, "Hunters!" as more windows exploded and another wave of thunderclaps from activated glyphs hammered Gabe's eardrums. Tentacles wormed their way into the house from every side.

Jackson snarled at the rest of them, glaring at Brett. "We wouldn't *have* to fight if *someone* had been more careful with the house's wards! The creatures of the Dawn should never have found us here!"

Brett looked down his nose at the smaller boy, and when another massive tentacle whipped out of the kitchen, Brett raised one hand and clenched it into a fist. Water burst forth from the sink, wrapped around the tentacle, and crushed it like a transparent vise.

Gabe grabbed Jackson by the shoulders. "We don't have time to argue! We need to concentrate on *not getting killed*!" He faced the rest of the group. "Let's get upstairs! The glyphs down here are done for, we're gonna get overrun!"

Brett nodded, and in the time it had taken Gabe to finish his last sentence, Lily had already started helping Kaz climb to the second floor. Brett, Jackson, and Gabe fell in right behind them.

At the top of the first flight of stairs, a hunter burst through an unbroken window. Every bit as hideous as the others Gabe had seen, the skinless, eyeless, earless beast was a ferocious bundle of fangs, claws, and violence—and Gabe's heart stood still as a water glyph sprang to life and froze the hunter solid with an earsplitting *CRACK*. The beast toppled from the windowsill to the hallway floor and shattered into thousands of sparkling golden shards, but before those shards had even come to rest, another hunter leaped through the same window. The creature wasn't alone: Gabe heard six other water glyphs activate from bedrooms along the length of the hallway. They were closing in from all sides.

Lily's eyes flashed and sparkled silver, and a small tornado picked the hunter up and flung it all the way to the far end of the hall, where it struck the wall and gruesomely ruptured, splattering golden goo and broken bits of its body from floor to ceiling. But door after door sprang open as more hunters appeared, and the entire house shook again and shifted what felt like three feet to the left.

"Unbelievable!" Jackson spat. "The beast with the tentacles has taken the house off its foundation!"

"Keep going up the stairs!" Gabe shouted. "We might be able to get out through a window!"

That was what Gabe and Jackson had done when they'd encountered the Eternal Dawn at Uncle Steve's university building. Jackson—much as Gabe disliked him, distrusted him, and found him unbearably irritating—had saved both their lives by conjuring a solid disk of golden magick for them to ride down to the ground. *No reason he can't do that again!*

Kaz spoke up. "Yeah, but how do we keep these things from following us?"

A hunter rammed through a bedroom door, sprang off the opposite wall, and launched itself toward Lily and Kaz. Gabe felt his eyes flare with heat as he held up one hand, fingers splayed, and conjured a solid wall of flame directly in front of the hunter. The beast struck the wall and roared as it ignited—but even though Lily and Kaz both flinched, all that reached them was a shower of fine ash.

Panting, Gabe slumped against a wall.

Lily, who was supporting a visibly weak Kaz, said, "I don't know how long we can keep this up."

Gabe nodded. "Kaz, can you bring up some sort of barrier? Block them in?"

"If I do, it'll wreck what's left of the house."

Jackson put a hand on Kaz's shoulder, his eyes solid glimmering gold. "Argent Court is lost, Kazuo. Do what you must." From the site of Jackson's touch, golden energy washed over and through Kaz, and his own eyes turned solid slate gray. Jackson was using his magick to boost Kaz's earth power. He'd done that for all of them in the past. To Gabe, it felt kind of like being hooked up to a battery. *No . . . more like being hooked up to a power plant.*

Kaz raised both his hands, and with a violent rumble a broad slab of bedrock erupted through the floor between them and the advancing hunters. Where the hallway had been, now they could see only a rough sheet of stone.

Kaz's eyes turned brown again as he slumped against Lily. "Wow, that was a lot harder than it should have been. Having a magick doppelganger running around really takes it out of you."

"Keep going up!" Brett said.

Gabe and Lily grabbed Kaz to support him as they climbed

two more flights of stairs, until they stood in the fourth-floor hallway. "Okay," Gabe called out, "try to find a window with no hunters or tentacles. Jackson, you ready to get us out of here?"

Jackson opened his mouth to speak, but any words he might have said were lost as the sound of splintering, shattering wood and stone filled the air around them. Tentacles burst through windows, through doors, straight through walls, and then the *entire roof of the house* ripped free from its joists and disappeared, leaving the five of them gaping upward, exposed to the cloud-clotted sky.

Except . . . it wasn't the sky they were looking at.

Something hung there, above the house, and as they watched, its color rippled and changed from gray to putrid, oozing gold.

It is *like the thing from Greta's room!*

It seemed to have the same camouflaging abilities of the monster at the hospital, but it was much bigger. Gabe craned his head back, and back, and *back*, as he took in the sheer immensity of it. It took his brain a few long moments to process what his eyes were seeing.

The body of the oblong, bloated creature suspended in the sky overhead was easily the size of a blimp. A grotesque gelatinous hood covered its upper half, and the lower half was made up of broad, banded segments like an insect's exoskeleton. Protruding from the seam that ran along its perimeter, a mass of tentacles hung down. Two dozen. *Three* dozen.

At one end of the nauseating, unnatural body, eight gleaming golden orbs swiveled and twitched, and Gabe almost vomited. *Oh God. Those are eyes!*

Howls from the hunters reached them from the lower floors, and Gabe risked a look away from the sprawling, repulsive creature. When it tore away the roof, several interior walls had also crumbled, along with parts of the floors. Now Gabe stood ten feet away from a pit that plunged through the middle of the house. Edging forward, he could see all the way down to the ground floor.

Into the dining room!

All of Uncle Steve's and Greta's research was there, lying unprotected on the table—alongside the Emerald Tablet. Gabe forced his vocal cords to work. "The research! The Tablet! It's all still down there!"

Gabe couldn't tell if the blimp-like monstrosity overhead understood him, or if it had simply paused to catch its breath after demolishing the top floor of the house, but now it sent five mammoth tentacles surging at them with renewed energy.

No. Not at *them*. At *Gabe*.

But he already knew the tentacles were susceptible to fire, and though Argent Court's wiring had just been shredded along with most of the rest of the house, the tentacle creature had made a tactical mistake. By tearing the roof away, it had given Gabe a direct line of sight to the electrical transformer fixed to a pole down the street.

"Guys," Gabe breathed. "You might want to back up."

Crackling, blue-white energy arced out of the transformer, wreathed Gabe's body, and became roaring red-orange-white fire. He thrust his right hand upward, fingers spread, and lances of flame stabbed out from each finger, ripping and charring the blimp-creature's limbs. Its shell turned a brilliant yellow where the flames hit, the heat rippling away and deepening into waves of burgundy.

A bizarre sound quavered out from the monster. *Like whale song* . . . Except it made Gabe feel dirty. Contaminated. He wasn't sure if the creature was in pain or just furious.

"Get down there!" Gabe barked. "We've got to get the research and the Tablet!"

"We can't just leave you up here!" Kaz waved an arm weakly at the hovering creature. "You can't hold it off forever!"

Gabe took a deep breath and prepared to draw power again. "It wants me! So let me keep it busy! You'll have your hands full with hunters, anyway! Now go!"

He threw both arms in the air. A river of blinding electricity flared out of the nearby transformer, and this time Gabe didn't absorb it. His eyes ablaze with such heat that his friends had to turn their faces away, Gabe took the controlled lightning and bent it upward, and where the energy passed by his hands, it became fire.

Bloodred fire, which he sent crackling straight into the

creature's underbelly, where it carved a trench across the entire length of its body.

The creature screamed, and its tentacles withdrew back into its jellylike carapace with a wet, sucking sound that Gabe was sure he'd hear in his nightmares.

Gabe staggered. He turned and found Kaz, Lily, Brett, and Jackson all still standing there, gaping at him. "Okay, fine, we'll go together," he gasped. "Now let's *move!*"

Jackson created one of his golden disks of magick, and the five of them sank down through the ruins of Argent Court to the dining room.

"Kaz, gather everything up," Gabe said.

Kaz's hands were shaking as he collected Uncle Steve's and Greta's research into a big, messy pile. "Uh, Lily? Would you grab the Tablet, please?"

Lily nodded, but as she took a step toward the magickal book, two hunters burst through a weakened section of wall right in front of her. Gabe saw her eyes flash silver, and she caught one of the hunters in a whirlwind that slammed it into the ceiling with bone-crunching force. But the other hunter grabbed the Emerald Tablet in its jaws and bounded back the way it had come, out of sight.

"No!" Jackson shouted. "We must not lose the Tablet! *We must not!*"

From far above them, the blimp-creature's whale-song cry

penetrated all the way to Gabe's bones. An ooze-covered tentacle exploded through a pile of rubble, knocking Gabe flat.

Brett sliced through the tentacle with an icicle sharpened into a blade like a broadsword, but this left the full weight of the appendage to crush Gabe as it landed on him.

His ears rang. The tentacle lay like a fallen tree on top of him. He couldn't breathe.

Brett's voice at his ear said, "Come on, buddy, let's get you out of here," but those words sounded as if they were coming from the end of a very, very long tunnel.

The floor trembled underneath him. Brett staggered away, eyes going blue-green. *What's happening?*

His eyesight dimmed as he saw Jackson put a hand on Lily's shoulder, and her eyes flash into a silver so intense it left spots in his vision. Then the rest of Argent Court disappeared into a full-fledged tornado.

7

Lily's air power surged through her like a hurricane.

Enhanced by Jackson's pure magick, what would have been a stiff wind turned into a vortex of incredible power. The ruins of walls and furniture and monstrous Arcadian creatures churned around her like water circling a drain. But in the eye of the storm where she stood, all was quiet.

She felt hands yank at her, and the funnel of debris all around her began to slow.

"Lily, we have to get out of here!" Gabe screamed into her ear. As he pulled her away, she felt the air slip and then fall from her grasp.

The next thing she knew, Gabe and Jackson were hustling her along the street. They'd made it several blocks away from Argent Court and the Dawn's creatures weren't following, but still, Lily sensed that something was wrong.

"Wait," she said. "Where're Brett and Kaz?" She turned around looking for them, but Gabe and Jackson were the only ones in sight. "Brett!" she screamed, suddenly afraid. Where was he? Where was her twin?

"We got separated," Gabe whispered. "They were on the other side of the tornado, and then part of the ceiling fell down between us. But right now we have to move, Lil." He pulled her and Jackson onto a side street. "We'll be safe in the tunnels." He glanced around—on all sides of them, as well as up at the sky. "I hope they're okay." He sounded as worried as Lily felt. "I mean"—he glanced quickly at Lily—"I'm *sure* they are."

"As am I," Jackson said. "Unlike Argent Court." He turned to Lily. "I believe you destroyed what remained of my family's home."

"And took care of our little problem with that not so little monster-tentacle-blimp thing," Lily reminded him, a bit defensively.

Jackson nodded. "Yes. Regrettably, the tornado was quite necessary."

They came to a stop next to a familiar manhole. Lily remembered vividly the first time she'd ever seen it: the night she and Gabe and Kaz and her brother had found the Friendship

Chamber, hidden far beneath San Francisco, and performed what was *supposed* to be a silly pretend ritual.

Sometimes Lily wondered what her life would be like now if she had never said the words "*I am bound to Air!*" They echoed in her skull.

On the other hand, if she'd never gone through with the ritual, she wouldn't have been able to summon a tornado and knock the ever-loving crap out of that giant floating tentacle creature. Lily would have allowed herself a tiny bit of satisfaction at that if she weren't so worried about Brett and Kaz. "Okay, good idea. This'll at least get us off the streets."

Gabe clambered down the ladder, but Jackson balked. "Must we shelter in tunnels *again*? Surely there is somewhere else we could take refuge? Some locale that does not feature raw, flowing sewage?"

Lily scowled. "It's not that bad, and you know it. We'll be safe down there, and this is the best place to wait for Brett and Kaz to turn up. Just be careful where you step."

Jackson scowled at her but obeyed. She followed him down the ladder, but before her head dropped below street level, she risked a glance down the alleyway, toward an open patch of sky. She could still see the tentacle creature, though it looked tiny from this far away, as it floated out over the bay.

Toward Alcatraz. Toward the breach we tore in the barrier between here and Arcadia.

A voice drifted to her from the sidewalk, some random

passerby. "Did you see the size of that blimp? I wonder why it was over the city?"

Lily used a burst of air to close the manhole cover behind her and almost fell off the ladder in surprise when Jackson shouted from below, "I say, who is that? *Who goes there?*"

Lily hurried to the bottom of the ladder. Gabe lit a floating orb of flame, illuminating a badly startled Jackson standing a few feet away from Kaz, who was slumped on the ground and breathing hard. His overstuffed backpack rested beside him, with the edges of a few handwriting-filled pages sticking out of it. Kaz waved a supremely nonthreatening hand at Jackson, whose eyes had flared gold.

"Kaz!" Lily rushed to him. "Are you okay? Where's Brett?"

"I'm okay, yeah, I think. And—I thought Brett was with you guys?"

Gabe stepped closer. "You didn't see him after you left the house?"

Lily's stomach plunged. *Where's Brett?*

Kaz shook his head. "It was all I could do just to put one foot in front of the other." He peered up at Jackson. "Sorry, I didn't mean to scare you. I was going to wait for you guys in the Friendship Chamber, but I just got so *tired. . . .*"

Jackson composed himself and looked down his nose at Kaz. "I was most certainly *not* scared. I simply did not expect to trip over you."

Gabe offered Kaz a hand, but Kaz made a sorrowful face.

"If you could just maybe give me a couple minutes? That was a long walk. . . ."

Gabe eyeballed Jackson. "All right with you if we just chill for a second?"

Jackson made sure everyone could see his eyes roll before he turned his back on the group and wandered off down the tunnel.

"Don't go too far!" Lily called, and Jackson made an elaborately rude gesture at her by way of response.

"Sorry," Kaz said again. "I just need a sec to . . . catch my breath . . ." His eyes slid closed, and his breathing deepened.

Lily kept her voice low. "OMG. Is he *asleep*?"

Gabe nodded, looking amused. "Let's give him ten minutes." Gabe's eyes flashed brilliant green in the glow of his flames. "I just realized how strong Greta must've been. To be hooked up to the apographon, like Kaz is now, but still be able get to Argent Court and do all that work? Wow."

It was hard not to grin back when Gabe smiled. Lily would never have said it out loud, but she was *so* glad he hadn't ended up moving away to Philadelphia, the way his uncle had planned. Just the thought of it made her depressed.

Gabe divided his sphere of fire into smaller and smaller pieces, and soon the tunnel was lit as if by a swarm of hovering lightning bugs. They floated like lanterns. Or like bullets waiting to be fired.

Fire was beautiful, but it was also dangerous.

Lily's grin faded as her brain worked, ticking through thought after thought. Brett was still out there somewhere, probably in trouble, maybe hurt. And even though she felt safe from the Eternal Dawn down here in the tunnels, as much as she hated to admit it to herself, just being near Gabe made her feel vaguely uneasy.

How badly he burned that creature that tried to grab him . . .

What if—

What if Gabe ever lost control?

What if she or one of their friends ever got caught in one of those rivers of flame?

Maybe Brett could survive it, since he had bonded to water. Kaz, too, more than likely, if he could surround himself with earth fast enough. But her? *Air fuels fire.*

One slipup and she'd die screaming.

"I'm sure Brett's okay," Gabe said. He was looking at her, concerned.

The worry must have shown on her face, and of course, Gabe thought it was because Brett was missing—not because Lily was wary of his fire. Gabe reached out to her, but she pretended not to notice and took a step away. "I've . . . well. I've got to believe that. You know? And anyway, it's not like he hasn't been able to take care of himself since he came back." She tried for a smile. "We should probably be more worried about who-ever he runs into."

Gabe grunted in agreement. "Remember that wave he

pulled up, out on the island right after he got out of Arcadia? That thing was *massive*."

"Yeah."

Silence fell between them. It stretched out long enough to make Lily want to squirm. "That huge blimp creature," she murmured, so as not to wake Kaz. "It looked like it was heading for Alcatraz, didn't it?"

Gabe sat down, and after a moment Lily did as well. Close to Gabe, but not too close. He said, "Yeah. Between that and all those abyssal bats, and who knows how many members of the Dawn are out there . . . and we've lost the Tablet. After all we went through, now the Dawn has it."

"You think we'll be able to stop them?"

"From merging Arcadia with Earth?" Gabe asked. "From bringing back my evil ancestor, Jonathan Thorne? From using the energy from the breach to build an army?" Gabe sighed and took a long moment before he shrugged. "I think we *have* to." His lips twitched upward.

"What?"

He shook his head. "Nah, just a dumb thought I had."

"Tell me."

Gabe sighed. "It was just . . . it occurred to me. We're kind of like the Fantastic Four."

She raised an eyebrow. *He's trying to get me to think about something besides Brett.* It was a sweet gesture. She decided to go along with it. "Oh?"

"Well, I mean, think about it. You've got the Thing, who's obviously earth, right? And the Human Torch."

"Yeah, fire. Okay."

"The other two are a little harder, but what's the Invisible Woman if not air?"

"Gabe, you are *such* a nerd."

Their eyes met. Dark brown and green. Lily wanted to reach out and take his hand . . . even better, she wanted him to reach out and take hers.

"You say that like you didn't know it already."

Lily chuckled. "So you're saying the stretchy guy is water?"

"It *is* a stretch—ha-ha. But yeah, I mean, he sort of flows and takes different shapes like water. Why not?"

She peered down the tunnel, where Jackson stood, practicing his sulk. "So what does that make Ghost Boy?"

"I don't know. A giant pain the butt?"

Brett's voice echoed down the ladder from the manhole. "You guys do realize anybody up here can hear every word you're saying?"

Lily sprang to her feet, relief flooding her whole body. *"Brett?"*

Brett clambered down the ladder, and Lily bounded to him and threw her arms around him. *"Oh my God I'm so glad you're okay they didn't catch you did they are you hurt the rest of us made it!"*

Brett gently disengaged from her. "Okay, take a breath! I'm

fine. Had to ditch a couple of hunters, that's what held me up." He turned toward Gabe. "But seriously, what's the point of having a secret hideout underneath the city if you're just going to sit right here at the entrance?"

Kaz had awakened, and Jackson rejoined the group as he got to his feet. "That apographon! I feel like a dead battery!" Kaz said through a massive yawn. He stretched and yawned again. "Calling up that stone wall almost made me black out, and that was with Jackson's help."

Brett looked at each of them in turn. "The Dawn took the Tablet, didn't they?"

Gabe nodded bitterly. "Yeah. We screwed up big-time."

Brett closed his eyes, his face creasing in a pained expression. But when he opened them again, they glimmered with the ocean's deep blue-green. "So we've got to get it back. Before the Dawn revs up the evil. And listen, there's all those bats on Alcatraz, and it looked like that was where that giant flying yuck monster was headed. I'm betting that's where the Tablet's going to end up, too."

"Right," Gabe said. "That's what I was thinking, too. They're gonna use it on the breach. Split it wide open."

"It will amaze you," Jackson said, "but for once I am in total agreement."

"Okay." Lily raked a hand through her hair. "Okay. So we think we know where they're going, and we think we know what they're going to do, more or less. So what do *we* do?"

Brett shoved his hands in his pockets and showed them all his teeth. "I say we get to the bay and crash the Dawn's party. Just like they crashed your house, Jackson."

The tunnel lit with a faint yellow iridescence as Jackson's eyes turned solid glowing gold. "Yes," he said, not sounding like an eleven-year-old boy at all. "Yes, let's."

8

Gray light fought its way through the low-hanging cloud cover as the five of them made their way to the end of Pier 39. Gabe kept an eye on the restaurants and shops they passed by, but the overcast weather was keeping almost everyone inside. The only people in sight were two cops and a homeless man. The group hid from the police, but after they emerged and passed the man huddled on an unfolded cardboard box, Gabe dug out a crumpled five and gave it to him.

"God bless you, son," the man said through a straggly, yellow-white beard. Gabe figured he had to be at least seventy.

"You shouldn't be near the water." Gabe glanced out at Alcatraz, its bulky silhouette clouded by the distant swarm of abyssal bats. "It's dangerous today."

The old man nodded solemnly. "Okay."

A minute later, Gabe glanced over his shoulder and saw the man, folded cardboard under one arm, scurrying away up the Pier 39 concourse. *Maybe he'll be okay.*

I wonder if we will.

Gabe had no idea what was going to happen once they got to the island, but with the Eternal Dawn's creatures so thick around the breach, he didn't see any way for it not to be something terrible.

No one spoke as they reached the observation deck at the end of the pier. Flagpoles and coin-operated telescopes dotted the heavy railing, and Gabe leaned against it, staring out over the choppy gray waves. "No sign of the flying tentacle thingy."

"No, but . . ." Beside him, Lily touched his arm and pointed.

Standing near Gabe's shoulder, Kaz said, "Wow. Subtle." Jackson snorted. Brett stayed silent.

Lily was pointing at a yacht making its way across the water, straight toward Alcatraz. Gabe didn't know much about yachts beyond what he'd learned from a few minutes of a show on the Travel Channel, but it was obvious that the sleek, white, futuristic craft was a million-dollar vessel. *Or two million. Or ten. It looks more like a spaceship than a boat.* Gabe figured it had to be forty feet long. The kind of thing super-rich people would throw parties on and show off for the rest of the world.

What really caught his eye, though, and what must have

grabbed Lily's attention right off the bat, was the name embla-zoned on the stern: *Arcadia.*

Kaz was right. *Subtle.*

"That boat belongs to the Dawn, right?" Lily turned to face the rest of the group. "I mean, it has to. So what do we do?"

Jackson looked as if someone had shoved a whole lemon into his mouth. "Clearly we need to reach that craft. The odds are excellent that the Emerald Tablet is aboard it."

Gabe nodded. "Yeah. And we need to try to get it back before the yacht reaches that." He waved a hand toward the island. "That *wall of bats.* Brett? Can you do that invisible-water-shield thing again? So they don't see us coming?"

Brett's eyebrows quirked. "Here? On the ocean? You better believe I can."

Gabe looked at Lily and Jackson. "Then we just need trans-portation. Which of you wants to give us a lift?"

"Oh." Lily drummed the fingers of one hand on her upper arm. "I could get us there, but the wind might disrupt Brett's illusion thing. I don't know . . ."

Jackson grunted. "Yes, yes, leave it to me to be the linchpin of this entire enterprise." He shouldered past Lily and Gabe and climbed the low fence, perching on top after he'd swung his legs over. "Mr. Hernandez, I suppose I have no choice but to ask you to do the honors."

Brett sneered at Jackson as he climbed over the railing. "Yeah. Everybody get close." Gabe, Lily, and Kaz clambered over, and as the five of them clustered together, Brett summoned a shimmering sheet of liquid up from the waterline. It surrounded them and rose into a familiar cylindrical shape as Jackson conjured a broad, flat disk of golden light.

"You may talk if you must," Jackson said, gesturing everyone onto the disk. "But mind your balance. Should you be so foolish as to fall off, you will be on your own."

"All aboard," Gabe said. It came out more solemnly than he'd meant it to. They all stepped onto the disk with Jackson, Brett getting on last, and as the shimmering cylinder closed around them, Gabe knew that the five of them had just disappeared from view.

"Very well," Jackson said tightly. "Off we go."

They skimmed across the bay, only a few inches above the water. Gabe was pretty sure he could feel it each time a whitecap brushed the disk's underside.

"God, I can't believe this," Kaz muttered.

Lily said, "Can't believe what?"

"That we're all just *okay* with this. Hey, look, there's a ship controlled by the Eternal Dawn, a bunch of people who want to kill us. And it's heading straight toward, like, every abyssal bat ever. You know what would be a great idea? If we sneaked out there and climbed on board! When did this happen to us? When did we start saying, *Hey, let's go put our lives in danger! It'll be great!*"

Lily smiled but couldn't seem to think of anything to say.

Gabe tried for a grin, but it didn't feel right, so he went for earnest instead. "We started saying that when we found out the world would end if we didn't."

"Yeah," Lily said. "That pretty much sums it up."

As they skimmed farther into the bay, Gabe sensed something strange. It was hard to describe, but it felt like a pull, reaching out to him across the water. "Guys . . . do you feel that?" He strained his eyes, staring at Alcatraz's shoreline. "From the island?"

"I believe it is emanating from the breach," Jackson said without turning his head.

The breach. The breach Gabe had caused. It felt like a hole in the world. A hole with slick, steep sides that he would surely fall into if he got too close.

"Get ready, everyone," Brett murmured. "We're almost there."

Gabe dragged his gaze away from the island and concentrated on the yacht. Brett was right. At the speed Jackson was carrying them, they'd reach it in less than a minute.

Lily said, "Well, I don't see anybody on board. That's a little weird."

Kaz shrugged. "I was watching the bats."

"The yacht's probably got some kind of ward on it," Brett said. "Like the ones your uncle and Greta drew everywhere. We should be extra careful."

Jackson guided the golden disk up to the side of the yacht

and whispered over his shoulder, "Does anyone see any wards?"

Gabe scoured the boat for any trace of fire, but he didn't detect anything. The rest of them either shook their heads or muttered, "No." Jackson nodded and slowly began to raise the disk, lifting them up toward the railing. As he did, voices drifted down to them, and Gabe grabbed Jackson's arm, making a *hold on a minute* gesture. Jackson frowned but kept the disk where it was, so they could all listen but still be out of sight from whoever was on deck.

Gabe recognized Primus's voice immediately.

"Wretched little trolls." She practically spat the words out. "But they won't be a problem much longer. They may have defeated our leviathan, but now that we have the Emerald Tablet? Well."

Lily touched Gabe's shoulder. She mouthed the word at him: *Leviathan?*

He leaned close to her, his lips almost brushing her ear. "Must be the giant tentacle monster."

Above them, Primus went on. "Soon we'll use the Tablet to widen the doorway between here and Arcadia. We will build a glorious army of Arcadian creatures. With them, we will be unstoppable. The children will fall before us, as will all others who dare oppose us."

A male voice answered her: "For the glory of the Eternal Dawn!"

Gabe gestured for Jackson to take them up. As the disk

lurched back into motion, Gabe put a hand on the yacht's hull to steady himself, and just as quickly he yanked it back. The hull felt warm—warmer than Gabe had expected, given the frigid waters it was cutting through.

"What's wrong?" Brett whispered. Gabe narrowed his eyes at the hull, unsure of how to answer. *Something isn't right. . . .*

"Primus will most likely have the Tablet, so you should all prepare yourselves for a fight," Jackson said, his eyes shining gold as they settled on Kaz. "Well, those of you who aren't entirely useless."

Kaz's shoulders slumped. Gabe would have said something to Jackson about being nicer to Kaz, but just then he saw an odd flicker in the air around the hull.

What's going on here?

The disk lifted over the yacht's rail and settled onto the deck. Gabe opened his mouth to say, "Wait a second," but Brett had already leaped off the disk, eyes blue-green and ready. Gabe felt his own eyes flash into flame as he prepared himself to summon fire.

But the yacht's deck was empty.

Kaz glanced around, looking nervous as a rabbit. "Wait. Where is everybody?"

From the middle of the deck, Primus's voice rang out again. "Wretched little trolls. But they won't be a problem for much longer."

The sinking feeling that had begun when Gabe's hand

touched the yacht's hull gathered force in his stomach. He spotted the source of the voice: a set of large speakers in the middle of the deck. The prerecorded words continued, exactly as they had while they'd been listening from below. Gabe strode toward the speakers, *stomped* toward them. He felt his teeth grind and fire glimmer in his eyes.

The speakers erupted in flames. Cloth charred, and plastic quickly turned to black molten sludge. Gabe whirled to face his friends, all of whom had followed after him. His flare of anger quickly transformed into fear. "It's a trap! We need to get out of here!"

The word "here" hadn't even fully left Gabe's mouth before the entire yacht bucked beneath their feet. Gabe fell hard to one knee and saw Kaz crash into Lily and Jackson, knocking them over. Brett lurched but stayed upright, and he stumbled to Gabe's side.

"What's going on?" Kaz shrieked, but before anyone could answer, the truth made itself horribly clear.

The broad planks of the deck widened farther, their color changing to translucent gold as the ichor of the Eternal Dawn's creatures seeped across them. From around the yacht's perimeter, enormous tentacles sprang from the hull and curved inward, reaching.

The leviathan had never disappeared.

It was right here. Camouflaged, like the creature from Greta's hospital room.

They were *standing on it.*

With a wet, nauseating sound like a side of beef being torn in half, a ragged mouth yawned wide, spanning the width of the deck and separating Gabe and Brett from Lily, Kaz, and Jackson. Gabe got back to his feet and started sizing up the jump they'd need to take to get across it, but then the mouth sprouted overlapping sheets of daggerlike *teeth*. Vertigo almost overtook Gabe as he gazed down into its massive, reddish-brown, slime-coated gullet. He backed away from it as fast as he could, dragging Brett with him.

From the other side of the leviathan's gaping, gnashing mouth, Lily screamed, "Gabe! Brett! *Look out!*"

Gabe didn't even try to look behind him. He just threw himself to one side, barely avoiding the massive tentacle that skidded across the deck where he'd been standing. Brett stood his ground. A thick column of water arced up over the side of the leviathan's body and split into a whirling cage of translucent blades around Brett. One of the tentacles touched those blades and jerked back, golden ooze sprouting from a dozen deep lacerations.

The leviathan roared, its twisted, corrupted whale song penetrating Gabe's flesh and bones. It was so loud, Gabe thought his skull might explode.

"Gabe! Brett!" That was Kaz, screaming from the other side of the creature's maw. "The tentacles—it's trying to push us into its mouth!" Kaz yelped and ducked behind Lily as one of the monster's limbs reached for them. Lily's eyes gleamed silver-white, and a thunderous gust of wind blasted the tentacle back into the water. Jackson hurled golden disk after golden disk at half a dozen others—but it was just like the fight at Argent Court. No matter how many they battered, cut, or bludgeoned, the monstrosity just grew more.

They had to try, though. Gabe called up a scorching maelstrom of flames around him. If the creature couldn't get through Brett's blades of water, maybe it couldn't get through a wall of fire, either. Gabe raised his hands, and the fire rose up into a dome around him. Sure enough, when one of the tentacles swiped at him, it jerked back, slimy flesh charred and blistered.

But then two more arched high into the air, paused, and came hammering down at Gabe like a pair of pile drivers. Gabe screamed and dived out of the way as the boneless appendages smashed through the fire dome and into the leviathan's chitinous plating. *Those would have crushed me flat, flames or no flames! Why isn't my fire as powerful as Brett's water?*

Gabe had no time to figure it out. The sky overhead darkened, the sound of flapping, membranous wings reached his ears, and Gabe looked up to see at least two dozen abyssal bats heading their way. No—they were heading straight at *him*, ignoring everyone else, and for a moment he feared he might lose control of his bladder.

It wasn't his imagination. Gabe had no time to check what

was happening to his friends because the sleek, eyeless, horrifying creatures began to dive-bomb him, one after another. Gabe scrambled to avoid their snapping jaws and thrusting, knife-blade talons. The leviathan seemed to have withdrawn to give the abyssal bats room to attack. *They're trying to kill me! Just like they killed Greta!*

The memory of Greta Jaeger, and what one of these creatures had done to her, supercharged the fire in Gabe's heart. Between one breath and the next, the world seemed to slow down. Everything around him ground to a halt until Gabe was the only thing moving in the entire world.

No . . . *no!* That wasn't true at all.

Everything was moving, all around him. Moving *constantly.* Moving at the molecular level. The *atomic* level. The tiny, sub-microscopic particles that made up matter itself. He could feel them, spinning in their infinitesimal orbits, the components of the universe—the protons, neutrons, and electrons that made up the flesh of the leviathan, the horrid skin and bone of the abyssal bats, even the air they all breathed.

Gabe remembered one of the homework sessions Uncle Steve had helped him with. *At absolute zero, there is virtually no molecular motion. But as that motion speeds up, what do you get?*

Heat.

Gabe reached out and took hold of those molecules. *Faster.* He felt them begin to speed up. *Faster. Hotter.* A voice, now familiar, spoke inside his head: *burn . . . burn . . . burn!* But

Gabe clamped down on that voice. It wasn't going to control him. Not this time.

He was the one in control.

And he didn't need any source of electricity anymore.

The spinning water blades nearest to Gabe hissed and turned to steam. Brett gaped at him and backed away as the air on the deck warped and quivered. Gabe raised eyes like the hearts of two volcanoes toward the abyssal bats overhead, and a ring of white-hot fire roared into life around him, rising and expanding.

Two bats hit the ring and vaporized.

The rest of them shrieked and circled, diving and rising. Gabe lifted his arms and the white-hot inferno grew larger, gaining intensity. Three more bats crashed into it, and they vaporized just as instantly as the first two.

I can do this. I can do this! I can clear out all the bats and then burn this freak leviathan out from under us! I CAN TAKE ON THE DAWN AND CLOSE THE BREACH!

Gabe splayed his fingers, sending tongues of flame shooting up, targeting individual bats—

And then the world turned blurry and cold.

Huh?

To his horror, Gabe watched the blazing ring of fire choke and die.

What's happening? What's doing this to me?

He took a breath, about to call out for his friends, but there was something wrong with his throat. The fire gone, the flame in his eyes snuffed out, Gabe gasped for air.

He couldn't get any.

I can't breathe!

Gabe's hands flew to his throat as the blurred, distorted world around him faded to darkness.

9

Between the giant flailing tentacles and the diving, scream-ing abyssal bats, Lily could barely keep track of where she was on the leviathan's shell, much less watch out for all the others.

One gust in the wrong direction and I'll push somebody into the bay by accident! And using her command of air to shove the creatures away from her was getting harder as more and more of them attacked.

"Kaz!" she screamed, glancing over her shoulder, "On your left!"

Kaz squealed and threw himself flat as the talons of an abyssal bat whooshed by just above his shoulder blades. "How are we supposed to fight something we're *standing on?* We're like fleas on a giant dog! One good scratch and we're history! Lily, we've got to get off this thing!"

Easier said than done, with Gabe and Brett all the way on the other side of that giant gross mouth.

Kaz got back to his feet but huddled between Lily and Jackson, trying and mostly failing to use his backpack as a weapon. *He's not moving fast enough . . . !* Lily grabbed Kaz's arm and wrenched him out of the path of a blackened, smoking abyssal bat that crashed hard into the spot where he'd just been standing.

"Holy crap! What happened to that thing?" Kaz cried, staring in fascinated horror as the creature crumbled into glowing, charred chunks.

As if in answer, a blast of heat reached them from the other side of the leviathan's broad, fang-filled mouth, and Lily caught a glimpse of Gabe through the bat-winged swarm. A churning circle of fire surrounded him. "I think Gabe happened to it!"

Lily looked away, trying to hide her worry. She hoped that the Dawn's creatures were the only things that ended up as blackened husks.

She didn't have time to worry, anyway—not while she, Kaz, and Jackson still had their own Arcadian monsters to contend with. She shunted another tentacle away with a pulse of wind. Her lips quirked upward as the out-of-control limb slammed three abyssal bats out of the sky.

Jackson sent a spinning golden disk into the densest part

of the attacking bat swarm, but the beasts scattered before it could do any damage. He threw a contemptuous look at Kaz. "Surely you can do something besides wish ill will at these horrors, Kazuo? What happened to 'I am bound to Earth'?"

"It's Brett's stupid apographon!" Kaz snapped and swung his backpack at another abyssal bat. "I'd have a hard time finding stones to use out here in the middle of the ocean on my best day, but now?" He grunted and ducked under a leathery wing. "I'm not much better than a paperweight!"

Lily saw two bats heading straight for her, and she surprised herself by taking in a great breath and *blowing* at them. A gale-force wind rushed from her lungs, sweeping up both creatures and slamming them into each other. They fell into the water in a shrieking tangle of wings and talons.

Panting, Lily noticed that the fierce wave of heat Gabe had generated had abruptly disappeared, but before she could turn her head to see what was going on, Brett crashed into the ichor-covered surface at her feet with a thunderous impact—a circle of golden energy binding his arms to his body.

In horror, Lily dropped to her knees by Brett's side. Her twin's eyes were closed, but she could see him breathing, and she couldn't find any blood anywhere. *He's just knocked out. Please let him just be knocked out!*

She tried to figure out where the energy circle had come from, and traced a shimmering line of magick from it to . . . Jackson?

The pale boy scowled at Brett, his smooth face rendered aged and ugly by hatred. "What are you *doing*?" Lily screamed in shock. *Why attack Brett just when we need him the most? Why attack Brett AT ALL?* "Let him go!" In her voice, Lily heard the roar of a hurricane.

"Not a chance," Jackson said, icy calm. "He's betrayed us."

Lily's eyes went cold as her element surged, and she was about to tell Ghost Boy exactly what would happen if he didn't turn her brother loose, when Kaz's trembling voice shouted, "Guys, look out, look out, *look out*!"

Lily turned to see a huge abyssal bat, almost twice the size of the others, diving for her with its knife-sharp talons outstretched.

A volley of softball-sized golden orbs blasted into it like a load of buckshot. The bat screeched, knocked out of the air, and slammed hard into the leviathan's shell. Lily stared as it slid lifelessly into the bay below.

Jackson came and knelt beside her. His eyes blazed gold, and a transparent golden shell formed around the four of them. An abyssal bat slammed into it and bounced off, and Jackson hissed, gritting his teeth at the impact. "I cannot maintain this shield for long. You must provide us with our escape route."

For a moment, all Lily could do was stare at him. Jackson had just attacked her brother, but somehow he was still on their side?

"Oh God!" Kaz shouted. "Lily, look!"

She followed Kaz's line of sight. Nearing the island's shore, a cluster of abyssal bats held something in their talons. Something that looked like . . .

Gabe.

But there wasn't any time to do more than think his name. A shadow fell across them, and Lily whipped her head up to see a massive tentacle rising above them, stretching up to its full length. Jackson's voice in her ear took on a note of desperation. "Lily, please. Get us out of here."

Lily glanced at Brett, still motionless on the floor. Then she stood. As she did she felt silver-white air energy dance along her skin, out to the tips of her fingers. She took a deep breath.

It's up to me. I've got to get us away from here. Concentrate, Lily . . . summon the air . . .

The screeching of the abyssal bats faded away, along with Jackson's and Kaz's voices. Air was all that mattered. Air was everything. Another deep breath filled her lungs with the salty bay winds. It tasted so good. So *pure.*

How long has it been since I've needed my inhaler? The need for it seemed so far away now. As if she'd never had asthma in the first place.

Lily's hair ruffled in the wind.

The air spoke to her. Sang to her. Every current like a different voice, and all of them needed to sing together. She would guide those voices. Lead them. Conduct them like a massive symphonic choir.

Lily told the wind to encircle her brother and Kaz and Jackson and finally herself.

Are you ready to sing for me?

The voices answered her, trilling, cascading through her mind. *Yes, Lily. Let us sing. Hear our song. Feel it. Unleash it. NOW!*

Dimly, Lily was aware of the sudden, deafening roar of the wind as it swept them up and hurled them into the air, but to her it sounded like the most beautiful, heartbreaking melody. She saw the leviathan recede below them, its gargantuan shape dwindling as they rose higher and higher, but her head had filled with the song of the air. Lily never wanted to hear anything but that majestic music ever again.

Moisture ran down her cheeks as the booming breath of the wind carried them up into the thick gray clouds. The melody saturated her body, thrumming inside her bones.

I am one with the air. I am one with the wind. I am the sky!

Brilliant sunlight washed over them as they broke through the cloud cover, rocketing ever upward. Lily spread her arms and twirled, buoyed by the roaring, gusting wind. Her body was weightless.

I am the air. I am the wind. I will soar forever!

She touched her face, marveling at the ice crystals forming on her cheeks, and wondered in an abstract way why her lungs had begun to burn—

And she heard screaming.

Why would there be screaming? *Who* would be screaming, up here in the pure, free air? Soon she would reach the edge of the stratosphere, up where the blue faded into black, and she knew she could circle the Earth forever, skimming along the edge of the pure, perfect sky. Lily couldn't imagine a more glorious, peaceful existence.

Until Kaz grabbed her arm and screamed into her face. "Lily! We're too high! WE'RE! TOO! HIGH!"

Suddenly, the symphony of the air faded. Lily saw her unconscious brother, and Kaz and Jackson. They were so high up that Jackson had passed out, and Kaz's tears had frozen onto his face.

Lily gasped and felt the power of air slide from her grasp.

The four of them fell like rocks.

10

"LILY!"

Kaz's voice reached her, thin and nearly drowned out by the rushing wind. "Lily, you have to stop us!"

Lily couldn't breathe at all. Her lungs refused to work, and her stomach felt as if it were still somewhere up at the edge of space.

She had never been in freefall before. She didn't mind roller coasters, but she'd never gotten anywhere near those rides that took you up eight or ten stories just to drop you.

Now the wind was screaming past her face, and the tears in her eyes were crystallizing, and she realized part of the reason she was having a hard time hearing Kaz was that she was screaming, too, and had been since they'd begun falling.

Wild-eyed, she looked around. Far above her was Jackson, still passed out, and below him was Brett, also still unconscious. Kaz was closest to her, his arms and legs flailing.

I have to stop this. I have to stop this! But the falling sensation made it impossible to concentrate—and she knew she was about to die. She and all three of the boys were going to slam into the ground at hundreds of miles an hour, and there'd be so little left of them the police would have to mop them up with buckets.

Kaz's hand clamped down around her upper arm and pulled until they were face-to-face. "Lily! I'm not strong enough to help, and Jackson and Brett are both out! You've got to do it!"

They plunged into the clouds. Water droplets pounded into their skin, stinging like tiny needles.

"I . . . I can't! I don't know how! I can't *breathe*!" Her asthma had returned in full force, crushing her lungs, choking her.

The sky opened up as they dropped below the cloud cover, and San Francisco spread out below them, a deadly tapestry of concrete and steel.

Kaz grabbed her head with both hands. "I know you can! You're bound to air! You have to use your power, or there'll be no one to save Gabe—and the Dawn will win!"

Oh God. He's right.

I've got to do this.

I CAN do this.

I CAN DO THIS!

Kaz turned his face away from the sudden silver-white glare of Lily's eyes as they fell past the top floors of a skyscraper. Her voice thundered like a sonic boom: "I AM BOUND TO AIR!"

A cyclone twisted and shrieked below them, rising up around them, its walls thick with dirt and debris. Lily could sense all four of their bodies as the air found her and her friends, surrounding and cradling them as their velocity dropped, the speed draining away even as the walls of the cyclone kept them from being seen.

The twister slowed and dissipated as Lily, Kaz, Brett, and Jackson touched down in a vacant lot surrounded by a high chain-link fence. As soon as Lily's feet touched the ground, she rushed to Brett.

A tiny laugh escaped her lips when she saw his eyes flutter open. He sat up, rubbing the back of his neck. "Ow. My head hurts. Where are we? *Oof,*" he gasped as Lily crushed him in a hug.

"Everyone else okay?" she asked, releasing her brother.

Kaz just nodded at her as he sat and drew in huge lungfuls of air.

Jackson got unsteadily to his feet. "Good of you to bring us back down into the breathable atmosphere." He ran his fingers through his hair. "Why am I soaking wet? Oh. Right. Clouds."

Kaz stood up and looked around. "I think we're actually

about a block from my house. Good job picking a landing spot, Lily."

Lily spoke to Kaz as she helped Brett to his feet. "You're the reason we *landed* instead of going splat. You know that vintage Spider-Man poster you like so much in my room? It's yours." As Kaz grinned and blushed, Lily turned to her brother.

"Brett, are you sure you're okay?" She tried to think of what the symptoms of a concussion were. "Do you have a headache? Blurry vision? We can get you to a hospital . . ."

Brett stood and patted himself. "No. I think I'm okay. At least I will be." He whirled on Jackson and grabbed him roughly by his shirt. "Have you been working with the Dawn the whole time, Ghost Boy? Is that why you *attacked* me?"

"Release me, you fiend!" Jackson sputtered.

"Brett." Lily stooped to pull Brett off Jackson, trying to make her voice sound reasonable. There'd be a time and place to work out this problem between Brett and Jackson, but with Gabe in the hands of the Dawn, Lily knew this was not that time. "*Hermano*, enough with the fighting. The Dawn's got Gabe. We need to work together."

Brett shrugged off Lily's grip and jabbed a finger at Jackson. His gaze was as hard as ice, and his voice trembled with fury. "Gabe's going to have to wait. We've got this snake right here to deal with first."

Jackson stood up, wincing. His usually chalk-white face

was flushed. "*Me*? It was *you* who betrayed us all back there. Gabriel, especially."

"What are you *talking* about, you little—"

Lily moved to face Brett. "Hey! Did you hear me? They've got Gabe! We've got to go after him!"

"And I said *he could wait*!" Brett shouted.

Lily wasn't prepared for that. She took a quick step backward as if her brother had shoved her. Brett hadn't screamed in her face in—she couldn't remember how long. Not since right after Charlie died, when they were all a little raw and unpredictable.

Brett wasn't finished. "This little creep attacked me back there for no reason! You want to know why Gabe got grabbed up? Because of *him*!"

Traces of gold glimmered around Jackson's eyes. "That's a bald-faced lie! If you seek the serpent in our merry little band, look no further than Brett Hernandez! He was trying to *drown* Gabriel!"

Brett fumed and balled his hands into fists. "Oh, please. You've been plotting and scheming for a century, and *that's* the best lie you can come up with? I was trying to *save* Gabe from those bats, and I would have, too, if you hadn't lassoed me and slammed me into the deck!"

Lily knew Brett would never betray them, and as much of a wet blanket as he could be, she didn't think Jackson would, either. She was sure this was all some terrible misunderstanding, but they'd all need to calm down and listen to one another before they got to the bottom of it. "Guys, please—" she said, but they both ignored her. She glanced at Kaz and saw that he was on the verge of tears.

"Gabriel didn't need rescuing!" Jackson shouted. "He was about to incinerate the entire lot of them! But no, you surrounded him with water so he couldn't breathe, much less fight, and you just *watched* as the bats grabbed him up! I only wish I had acted faster. I might have saved him!"

"You know what I think?" Brett cried. "I think you didn't *want* to save him! You wanted him to get captured! That'd be some sweet payback for him trying to chuck you into Arcadia, wouldn't it?" When Jackson's eyebrows cranked up, Brett said, "You didn't think anybody else knew about that, did you? Gabe hoped that sending you in would bring his uncle back. I saw it happen from the other side!"

Lily felt a deep hole open up inside her. *Gabe wouldn't . . .*

"I need Gabriel to destroy Arcadia!" Jackson bellowed. "I need all of you! I want to destroy the Eternal Dawn more than anything! What do *you* want, Brett? What made you try to drown someone who is supposed to be your friend?"

Brett turned in a circle, rubbing his temples like all of this was giving him a terrible headache. Lily thought it looked like a gesture their dad would make—not her thirteen-year-old brother. Then suddenly he stopped and pierced Lily with a fierce look. "Lil, you don't believe him, do you? You know I'd never hurt Gabe! I'd never hurt any of you!" Brett cut his eyes toward Jackson. "Not even him. No matter how much I might *want* to."

Lily barely heard him. She was stuck on what he'd said about Gabe trying to push Jackson into Arcadia. Had Gabe really done that? . . . Was that why the ritual on Alcatraz went so wrong? That meant the breach was Gabe's fault! Pain speared through her chest, and she took several deep breaths.

She shook her head. They would have to get to the bottom of this later. The Dawn had Gabe, and she was sure they had nothing good planned for him. *The clock is ticking, so first things first!* This fighting between Brett and Jackson had to end, and she seemed to be the only one who could see that.

"You would have a difficult time hurting me, you honorless ruffian," Jackson said. Golden light burst across his irises as he closed in on Brett.

"Enough!" Lily shouted, and with a detonation of air, she knocked the two boys away from each other and back to the ground. "Look, Jackson," she said in a calmer voice. "I don't know exactly what went on back there on the yacht. I don't know what you saw, or what you thought you saw. But I do know that Brett would never have tried to hurt Gabe. And he sure wouldn't want Gabe to get captured."

"Yeah," Brett sneered. "We've got these things called contact lenses in the twenty-first century, Ghost Boy. Maybe you need some."

Jackson made a growling sound in his throat and appeared to be on the verge of speaking. Instead, he stood and stomped away from them, ripping a hole in the chain-link fence with a motion of one hand and a flare of golden light.

Kaz spoke up, dabbing at his eyes with the cuff of his sleeve. "Where do you think he's going?"

Lily shrugged. "Not far. We're the only people he knows." Unpleasant as he was, she couldn't help but feel bad for Jackson. Lily didn't think he'd betray them any more than Brett would. She and Kaz and Gabe and Brett were all he had.

How lonely that must be.

An idea seemed to occur to Kaz, and he started rummaging through his backpack as Lily turned to Brett. "We can't let him sulk for too long," she said. "We need to go after Gabe."

Brett nodded. "Absolutely. Now that the Dawn has both Gabe and the Emerald Tablet, they've gotta be planning to exchange Gabe for that founder guy. Just like they tried with Dr. Conway."

Lily shuddered as memories of the ritual in that gilded theater came back to her. The chanting cultists, the silver dagger, the blood cocoon spreading across Dr. Conway's body. *Is that going to happen to Gabe, too?* No. No, they couldn't let it. *She* couldn't let it. "Thorne. Jonathan Thorne. Gabe's great-great-great whatever."

"Right. And somebody that powerful? Who knows what he could do if they brought him to Earth. That could be the end of . . . well, everything. So, yeah. We go collect Ghost Boy and rescue Gabe, because as soon as we get Gabe back, the five of us can get rid of Arcadia once and for all. Destroy it."

Lily frowned and put a hand on Brett's forearm. "Hang on. Dr. Conway is still there. And Gabe's mom, too. You said you met her. What about them?"

Brett's expression darkened. "Nobody said it would be pleasant." Lily pulled back in shock, and he must have noticed, because his tone suddenly lightened a lot. "I mean, it might still be possible to get them back through the breach. I'm not saying we won't try. Of course we will."

Kaz spoke up. "Uh . . . guys? Speaking of getting rid of Arcadia and all, I figured I'd better make sure I still had everything we need for the ritual." He patted his backpack. "And, well, you know that ring, the one with Jackson's family crest? Yeah. It's gone."

Brett whirled around. "What do you mean, it's gone?" He snatched the backpack out of Kaz's grip and began to tear through it. "Where is it? Did you leave it back at Argent Court? Please tell me it didn't fall out somewhere while we were *in the sky*!"

"Brett, it's not like Kaz lost it on purpose! Calm down!" Lily said. "Just think, Kaz. Where's the last place you saw it?"

Kaz squinted. "Well, we were all in the dining room, talking about it, then the doorbell rang, and—oh no. Oh crap. Guys, I put it in the pocket of my hoodie!"

Brett frowned impatiently. "Okay. So where's your hoodie? We need that ring or the ritual won't work!"

"It's—I, uh. I gave it to the apographon."

Brett grabbed a double handful of his hair and pulled it, squeezing his eyes shut and gritting his teeth. Kaz looked totally crestfallen, and Lily put an arm around his shoulders. "It's okay. What matters is that we know where the ring is. Once we rescue Gabe, we'll come back and get it."

"No," Brett spoke flatly. No room for discussion. "We get the ring now."

"But, Brett, Gabe is—" Lily started.

"Like Kaz said, we're only a block from his house. We're getting the ring first. Right now."

There was no arguing with him. She could tell. Lily didn't like it, but she nodded.

They trudged in an uncomfortable silence that made Lily extremely relieved when she spotted Kaz's house ahead.

The Smith residence was a fairly big place, a stand-alone two-story home, but it definitely qualified as a "fixer-upper." Someone had been working on replacing some rotten planks on the front porch, and a hammer, box of nails, a saw, and two sawhorses still stood there beside the front door.

Jackson wrinkled his nose and said, "People actually live here?" and then, "Ow!" as Lily punched him in the shoulder.

"It's no Argent Court." Kaz sounded as if he were mustering

up every bit of pride he had. "But it's my house. You can sit out here on the curb if it offends you so much."

Jackson *harrumphed*, but he stayed with the group. Lily had been right—when Jackson had stormed off, he hadn't gone far. They'd found him standing in front of an electronics store, staring at the display of TVs. Now he walked along with the rest of them as they approached the Smith home.

"Come on," Kaz said. "Nobody ever goes in the front. And remember, nobody goes in *at all* until we figure out where Fake Kaz is."

Kaz led the way up the driveway, through a wooden gate, and along a path of stepping-stones through the grass to the rear of the house. Lily had been here many times before and knew there was a big picture window there that looked directly into the dining room. She couldn't begin to count how many dinners she and Brett had shared with Kaz's family. It was early afternoon, so everyone should be either at work or in school— but suddenly Kaz, a few paces ahead of her, hissed and threw his arms out, motioning for them all to stop.

"What is it?" she whispered. "What's wrong?"

Kaz's face had gone pale. He crouched down and crept up to the picture window, and Lily, Brett, and Jackson all followed suit. Lily peered over the edge of the windowsill, into the house, and her breath caught in her throat.

The Smith family—Kaz's mom and dad, and Kaz's little sisters, June, Kira, and Carlie—all sat at the dinner table, with what appeared to be a full-blown evening meal spread out in front of them. But none of them were eating. None of them were even moving, except to throw anxious glances at the doorway to the kitchen.

"What are we looking at?" Jackson whispered irritably. "Why are your relatives having supper at midday?"

Fake Kaz—the apographon—entered the dining room, carrying a big tray overloaded with mashed potatoes, green beans, and cranberry sauce. He still wore Kaz's hoodie. He set the tray down in front of Mr. Smith and, with a far-too-wide grin, said, "All right! Eat up!" The words were muffled through the glass of the window, but Lily heard them clearly enough.

Kaz groaned, "Oh no . . ."

Mr. Smith started to stand. Mrs. Smith, sitting next to him, grabbed his arm and tried to pull him back down. "Taylor. No. Don't."

Mr. Smith never took his eyes off Fake Kaz. "I have to." He pushed his chair back and stood. Fake Kaz stared at him as he did it, the eerie grin twitching at the corners. Mr. Smith said, "Enough is enough. You can't keep us here forever."

Fake Kaz's grin began to tremble. Lily sucked in a sharp breath as two translucent, shimmering heads vibrated out from Fake Kaz's, one on either side. One looked like Greta Jaeger. The other looked like Aria, Gabe's mother. Fake Kaz lifted his arms, and two other sets of arms sprouted from his torso, one above the real limbs, one below. The phantom limbs twitched and shook and *extended*, growing spindly and grotesque, their fingers stretching to horrible sharp points.

"No!" Fake Kaz shouted, in a voice made up of real Kaz's and Greta's and Aria's. "No! You sit down! *We will always be a family!*" One set of spindly, bony hands settled onto Carlie's shoulders. Kaz's littlest sister gave one wracking sob before she choked her tears off.

Lily stared in horror. Every personality that had occupied the apographon was manifesting at the same time—and that cluster of personalities seemed to have veered into madness.

June and Kira both started crying, and Mr. Smith slowly sank back into his chair.

What do we do? We have to do something! What do we DO?

From Lily's left, Brett hissed, "Where's the real Kaz?"

The back door of the Smith house slammed open. Before Lily could even react, she saw Kaz come charging through the doorway into the dining room, his hands encased in mounds of rock like twin wrecking balls. His eyes solid slate gray and shimmering with green power, weakness gone, Kaz screamed, *"Nobody makes my sisters cry!"*

Kaz slammed his hands together, catching the apographon's head perfectly between them.

The head exploded in a shower of splinters and fiery green sparks. Abruptly no more than a collection of broken stone and torn wire, any resemblance to Kaz or Greta or Aria disappeared in an instant. The ruined apographon collapsed to the dining room floor as a mess of rubble loosely wrapped in Kaz's hoodie.

The Smith family sat at the table, frozen. Stunned. Staring at Kaz.

Mr. Smith's eyes darted from Kaz's stone-encased fists to the ruined golem and then back again.

Kaz turned to face them, and let the rocks crumble and fall from around his hands. They landed in two neat piles beside his feet, and he shoved his now-clean hands into his pockets. "So, uh, hey, guys. How's it going? I mean, wait, no, don't answer that—I guess I already know." He sighed. "Listen, I've got to tell you a couple things, and believe it or not"—he glanced at the ruins of the apographon—"it gets kinda weird."

11

Gabe stood, silent, as his mother approached him. She was beautiful. She'd always been beautiful. His father thought so, too, and he told her so every chance he got. As she came closer and closer, Gabe realized how small he was. He barely came up to her waist, and when she bent down to hug him, she easily whisked him up off his feet.

Gabe wrapped his arms and his legs around his mother and buried his face in the side of her neck. He had so much time to make up for. So many long, sad hours spent missing her—missing the memory of her. Missing the *thought* of her. He'd forgotten the sound of her voice long ago.

Gabe hugged his mother tighter, and she chuckled. "You're such a strong little boy!"

Over his mother's shoulder, Gabe saw his dad grinning. He looked just like the photos Uncle Steve had shown him, except for one thing. His eyes were fire.

This . . .

. . . this isn't real.

Gabe barely even remembered his parents. How could they be with him now? Tears squeezed out of Gabe's eyes. Hot tears. *Burning* tears.

Heat washed over him as a ring of white-hot flames sprang up around the three of them. His mother's arms tightened, tightened, and her grip grew harder and harder, as if her arms were made of steel. Gabe tried to pull away from her, tried to see her face, but he couldn't. She held him locked in place and whispered in his ear, *"We will always be a family."*

The flames rushed inward. He felt them climbing his mother's body, and he knew the exact moment when they engulfed him, too. He was burning, they were all burning, skin and flesh scorching and charring, but it didn't hurt. In that moment, Gabe understood: the fire had taken everything.

And it wanted still more.

His mother loosened her grip just enough for Gabe to lean back and look her in the eye. Her face was already blackened, her skin cracking, and fire danced in her hair, but she smiled, and the pent-up love Gabe felt for her hurt as much as the flames. "No matter what, Gabe. We will always be a family."

Gabe's eyes opened, but just barely. His eyelids felt like they each weighed at least a thousand pounds, and it took every shred of strength he had to pry them apart. A roaring sound echoed through his ears, and after a few long, confusing seconds, he realized it was the sound of his own blood coursing through his veins. His arms and legs wouldn't move at all. It amazed him that he could even breathe. Panic threatened to overwhelm him, and he let his eyes close again while he fought it down.

I've been drugged.

Another slow, laborious exertion let him take a look around, even though his eyes were the only parts of him he could move, since his head refused to turn. He was in the back of a van, lying on a hard, cold metal floor. Whoever had taken him didn't care about how pleasant his trip was going to be.

Whoever took me . . . He knew exactly who. Thinking back, he remembered the sensation of the abyssal bats' talons, hooking under his limbs. But before that . . .

What had happened? Back on the yacht—the leviathan. One minute he was incinerating abyssal bats, and the next . . . *Nothing. All dark.*

Gabe might not have been able to move his body, but he

could still use his mind. He let his eyes close again and concentrated. He tried to recall the sensation he'd felt there on the deck, the grasp of molecular motion. The beauty and symmetry and *understanding* of the world that had let him summon the fire.

I can't move, but I can still burn this van to cinders!

He reached for his power and immediately suffered an excruciating crash, as if his mind had just slammed into a brick wall. His pathway to fire had somehow derailed and thudded to a dead stop.

What is this? What's happening?

Panic reared up again. Gabe reached out with his mind, tried to touch the fire . . . and couldn't. As if from a great distance, he became aware of a burning cold around his wrists, a cold so intense he could imagine it destroying his skin. Suddenly he was glad he couldn't move his head to see what shackled him.

The Dawn had clearly done something to him to prevent him from using his elemental power. *Anti-elemental chains?* The thought terrified him. *If they can cut me off, then they could do the same thing to everybody else!* Their elements were the only tools he and his friends had that gave them even the slightest chance of defeating the Eternal Dawn. And now he discovered that they could just be *neutralized*? Gabe shuddered.

As he pulled back on his attempt to summon his power, the cold on his wrists faded as well. Growing desperate, Gabe concentrated on what else he could feel and hear, in the hopes that he could learn something—anything—that might be useful.

Okay, I can tell we're moving. And I can hear traffic, so we're not on Alcatraz. Where are they taking me?

A voice spoke from the front of the van that chilled him in a completely different way than the shackles. He hadn't heard it many times before, but he felt as if he knew it as well as he knew Brett's or Kaz's or Lily's voice.

Cool and businesslike, Primus asked, "How much longer?"

Gabe's head was close to the front seats, with his feet pointed toward the van's back door, and Primus's voice came to him from over his left shoulder. So she was in the passenger seat. Another female voice answered her from the driver's seat—one Gabe didn't recognize. The speaker sounded younger than Primus. *Must be one of her followers.*

"We're about twenty minutes out."

"Think of it. How close we are! Soon we shall change the world!" An ugly kind of joy filled Primus's words. "The possibilities are endless, literally *endless*. The things we will accomplish with magick unbound!"

"Dvai shviunta," the driver said, and the words made Gabe's ears buzz and itch as if they were suddenly filled with ants. "Two worlds!"

"Yes. Two worlds combined into one perfect utopia. Once Thorne returns, and Arcadia and Earth are merged, can you imagine the praise we'll receive? The gratitude the rest of humanity will show us, once they realize what we have accomplished? The true Eternal Dawn will illuminate the world forever!"

The driver paused, and Gabe got the feeling she had turned to look over her shoulder. "And we're sure this boy is one of Jonathan Thorne's direct descendants?"

"Yes. That's not an error we'll make twice. We'll use him to remedy the mistake we made with his uncle, and finally return Lord Thorne to us. Now that we have the Emerald Tablet, the combined sacrifice will fulfill our destiny. Our struggle over the last century will finally bear fruit!"

Gabe's insides shriveled. They were going to sacrifice him just like Uncle Steve, return their deranged founder back to San Francisco, and then merge this world with the hellscape of Arcadia.

So is this it? Gabe wondered. *All this, and we've failed?*

No! He couldn't accept it. Couldn't even let himself think it.

"Um." The driver paused again. "I'm sorry . . . 'combined sacrifice'?"

Primus spoke with what sounded like a rare bit of patience. "Yes. The boy and the Tablet."

"You mean, we're sacrificing the Tablet, too? Mom, you can't be serious!"

Mom? The driver was Primus's *daughter*?

Primus sighed. "You're new to the Dawn. And I make

allowances where I can. But you *must* learn to have faith in my direction. All right?"

"It's not that I doubt what you're saying, Mom, I'm just trying to understand. The Dawn's been searching for the Tablet *forever*, right? And now we have to give it up? It's . . . I thought it was irreplaceable. All the wisdom it contains! All the power!"

"It is true that the Tablet will be destroyed as part of the ritual. But it isn't irreplaceable. Everything casts a shadow, Eva."

Eva. Gabe filed the name away.

"I . . . um." Eva seemed to be choosing her words very carefully. "I thought the Tablet didn't cast a shadow, though."

"Not in this world."

"So you're saying there's a second book of power?" Wonder filled Eva's words. "And it's in Arcadia?"

"There is. Yes. A shadow tablet for a shadow city. The Mirror Book." Primus's voice brimmed with excitement. "It is easy to forget how vast and strange the universe truly is, Eva. Just imagine the wonders Lord Thorne will show us when he returns! Doesn't it fill you with joy?"

Utterly helpless as the van sped to the site of his sacrifice, joy was the last thing Gabe could imagine feeling.

12

"I don't understand," Noriko Smith said for the fifth time. "You're an . . . an elementalist, like your friends, and you're facing a doomsday cult that wants to combine San Francisco with some . . . other dimension called Arcadia? And that's supposed to end the world? Kaz, I *don't understand*!"

She and her husband, Taylor, sat perched on the edge of the couch in their living room, while Kaz paced back and forth in front of them, rubbing the stubble on his scalp and making repeated false starts in his efforts to explain what was going on. Kaz's younger sisters, after loud and lengthy protests, had been sent upstairs to their rooms.

"I don't know what I can do to help you with that, Mom."

Kaz stopped and knelt in front of his mother, taking her hands in his. "Listen, nobody knows better than I do how totally, utterly bonkers this all sounds. But you've got to believe me. You're in danger. The whole city's in danger. You need to take Kira, June, and Carlie and go somewhere a long way from San Francisco. Like Chicago. Or maybe London. Do you know anybody in Australia?"

"But it's just ridiculous!" Mr. Smith shook his head and squeezed his eyes shut. "You're asking us to believe things that are patently impossible! I don't know what that thing was that looked like you—I suppose it must have been some kind of, of *robot*, and yes, that was very impressive when you hit it with rocks, but—son, you're talking about other dimensions! If even the scientists at the Large Hadron Collider haven't been able to prove anything like that, do you see where it's a little difficult to just take the word of my twelve-year-old son and his friends?"

"Right." Mrs. Smith sniffed. "It could've been holograms. I know about holograms. They're getting very advanced these days."

"It's not holograms or robots or even mutants or clones, okay? Trust me on this!" Kaz looked desperately from his mother to his father.

"Well, whatever it is, why are you involved?" Mrs. Smith asked. "How could this have happened? And if the city really is in danger, then you have to come with us! You're just a child, Kaz!"

Lily watched from the doorway of the dining room as the Smith family tried to make sense of what their son was telling them.

Good luck. I barely understand it myself, and I'm a way bigger part of it than you guys. She'd volunteered to help explain the situation to the Smiths, but Kaz had said he spoke the same dialect of science nerd as his parents and thought he'd have a better shot at doing it himself. Lily certainly understood how important it was for Kaz to convince them, but impatience was about to eat her alive. *Who knows where Gabe is now? Who knows if he's hurt?* They needed to be out looking for him, not having a family meeting.

Brett sat at the dining room table, about as far from Jackson as he could get while still being in the same room. He stared out the big picture window, wiggling one foot propped on the opposite knee. *He looks as anxious to get out of here as I do.* Jackson drifted around near Lily, occasionally glancing into the living room.

"The man is right about one thing," Jackson grumbled. "This *is* ridiculous. We should be on the move."

Softly, Lily said, "Just give Kaz a little time. It's his family. He owes them an explanation."

In the doorway, Jackson hissed, "*Ugh*, what a family of dolts."

Lily spun around to face him. She wasn't sure if it was Jackson's sheer lack of sympathy or the fact that she'd actually been starting to feel bad for him earlier, but his callousness made something inside her snap. She grabbed a big handful of Jackson's shirt and half-pushed, half-dragged him into the kitchen, where she pinned him in a corner in front of the microwave. As they went, Jackson squirmed and said, "Unhand me! This is an outrage!"

Looking around to make sure no one had followed them, Lily kept her voice low but put her nose close to Jackson's. "What is your *problem*?"

Jackson frowned but had the good sense to match the volume of his voice to hers. "I'm sure I don't know of what you speak."

Lily let go of his shirt but didn't back off. "Of *what* I *speak* is the fact that you constantly go out of your way to be as big a jerk as possible! You insult us, you make fun of us, you call us stupid. You just . . . you just *suck*! You don't *have* to be a creep, Jackson! What gives?"

Jackson's eyes had gotten wider and wider as Lily spoke. When she finished, he straightened his shirt and moved to step around her. "I have no obligation to explain myself to you."

Lily raised one hand, and a small, concentrated burst of wind blew Jackson right back against the counter. He winced at the impact and his eyes glimmered gold, but when he saw the expression on Lily's face, he stopped resisting. Lowering his gaze, he gritted out, "You wouldn't understand."

Lily let the wind fade. She stepped back and folded her

arms across her chest. "I'm a straight-A student. I won the science fair last year. I understand lots of stuff, Jackson. *Try me.* Is it because you miss your friends? Never got to say good-bye to your favorite pet? *What?*"

Jackson's gaze darted around as if looking for an escape route, but only halfheartedly. He sighed. "All right . . . all right. Since you insist so stridently."

Lily stood there waiting for a good ten seconds. "Well?"

Jackson looked up at her. At first she didn't recognize the emotions she saw in his eyes, but finally she realized he looked *scared*. She'd never seen him show an ounce of fear before. The closest he'd ever come was irritation.

"Miss Hernandez, when I was eleven years old, my father . . . *my own* father drugged me and chained me to a stone slab, and then he allowed a man named Jonathan Thorne to plunge a silver dagger into my chest."

Lily heard herself gasp. "Thorne, that's the guy who founded the Eternal Dawn."

Jackson nodded. "Killing me was the blood sacrifice Thorne required to create Arcadia, but Arcadia was not where I arrived. Instead I was sent to the Umbra, a realm outside of this reality. I was alone there, Miss Hernandez, with nothing but my mind and the tricks it played on me. I was trapped there for *eleven decades.*" He exhaled a long, slow breath. "You cannot imagine what it was like. The isolation. Staggering, *overwhelming* isolation."

She blinked. That struck a chord in her. It reminded her of all the time she'd spent trapped indoors before they'd gotten her asthma under control. All the days she'd spent staring out the window, while Brett and Kaz played tag outside and threw a battered Frisbee back and forth.

"Jackson, I—"

He shook his head, cutting her off. "I could sometimes hear sounds. Occasionally even see people, and eavesdrop on their conversations. But this was another torment, for I could do no more than observe. So I watched. Through the dense fog of what ethers separated us, I watched everyone I had ever known or loved grow old, wither, and die. And these were only glimpses, you understand? I never saw enough to feel as if I were a part of their lives. The world left me behind. How much has civilization changed in the last hundred years, Miss Hernandez? The night Thorne sacrificed me, I rode in our horse-drawn carriage. And now . . . now!" His lips spread in a terrible, joyless grin. "I emerge into a world I can barely comprehend. Your technology, your culture, your speech. I may as well be one of Mr. Wells's Martians for all I understand about the world around me. And do you know what the *best* part is?"

Lily shook her head, overwhelmed by this massive, unexpected outpouring.

"The absolute, very best part is that I still look like a little boy. I look younger than you, Miss Hernandez, and yet I cannot help but see you as the tiniest of children! Imagine, if you would, your grandfather, no, your *great*-grandfather, in a body eleven years of age. Imagine how he sees the world; imagine all the experiences he has had. Imagine *his mind*. Now picture him cavorting about dressed like *this*"—he plucked at his T-shirt—"and try to understand how he would *feel*."

To her own surprise, Lily felt tears welling up. She thought of her late grandfather, her *abuelo*, with his deeply wrinkled, dark-brown skin. How he'd always smelled of the most delicious pipe tobacco, and how he'd strummed his guitar and sung her Mexican lullabies every time she was sick. The image of him in Jackson's place . . .

"Jackson, I hadn't thought about it like that. About *any* of it. I never thought of you as . . ."

"As an old man? No. And yet that is the cruelest joke of all, because I am *not*. An old man would have lived a life. An old man would have grown, and perhaps received an education, and secured gainful employment. An old man would have made friends, and fallen in love, and had his heart broken. Maybe even more than once. He would have started a family, and raised his children, and witnessed the birth of his grandchildren. He would have embarked upon a career, and tried his best to leave a mark on the world. . . . But what did *I* do? Nothing. *Nothing.* I was trapped. A prisoner. All that experience, all that . . . growing up . . . I never had that. Never had any of it. I see how you and Brett and Gabriel and Kazuo relate to one another, and . . . and I want—I would *like*—to be a part of it. But I may as well be of a different *species* for all I *understand* it." He covered his face with his hands, and his shoulders trembled. "What *am* I? I am no boy, yet neither am I a man! I have no one, no family, no means of support! No knowledge, no understanding of the world around me!" Jackson's hands dropped to his sides, but he kept his eyes closed tight. "All I have is a hatred of Jonathan Thorne and the Eternal Dawn for inflicting this hell upon me. That is why I am *unpleasant*, Miss Hernandez. I have had a very, very long time to perfect such feelings, and . . . and not much chance to try any others."

Lily wiped the tears away from her cheeks with her sleeves and, just as Jackson opened his eyes again, she pulled him close to her and wrapped her arms around him. "I'm so sorry, Jackson," she whispered. "I'm so sorry. I'm so sorry."

What if she had been locked away from her mother and father? Worse than that—betrayed by her father and sentenced to the kind of torment Jackson had struggled through? What if she'd been torn away from Brett? Lily's family hadn't just supported her . . . they had *shaped* her. Once she could manage her asthma, it would have been easy to remain the strange little girl who never went outside. But her mother had pushed her—gently, with love, but definitely pushed her—to break out of the habits that had been forced on her. Without her mother's encouragement, and her father's pride in her, would she ever have started running track? Would she ever have discovered her own strength? Who would she be if she hadn't been able to grow like that?

Who would I have become if I'd had to stay trapped in my room?

All the insults, all the rudeness, every horrible thing Jackson had said and done, all made so much more sense to her now.

Jackson struggled against her, but only for a moment. Lily thought he might have been simply tolerating the hug, until his arms crept up and encircled her. Timidly. As if he wasn't sure how to do this. He pressed his face against her collarbone, and she felt a tear slide down onto her skin.

Quickly, and without looking up at her, Jackson let her go and turned away and splashed his face with water from the sink. Wordlessly, Lily handed him a nearby hand towel. When he'd dried off, he propped himself on the counter with both hands, his shoulders tensing. "It would, in my opinion, be unnecessary to relate the details of what I told you to Brett, or Kaz. Or anyone . . . ever."

A smile found its way onto her lips. "Pinkie swear?"

Jackson frowned. "I do not know what that means."

Lily turned and leaned against the counter beside him. "I can tell it bothers you when you get called Ghost Boy. Right?" Jackson grunted. She took that for a yes. "Well, when I was seven, I, uh, I had to stay indoors for a while. Like, most of a year. You know what everyone started calling me? They called me Kermit the Hermit."

Jackson stayed facing the counter, but he turned his head enough to look up at her with one eye. "That must have been . . . um. Difficult for you?"

She ran her fingers through her hair. *He's making an effort.* "Tell you what. I won't say a word if you'll think about making an effort to be, maybe, a little nicer."

"I seem to recall telling you a few moments ago that I . . . have had very little practice at that."

"It's pretty simple. If you're talking, and the person you're talking to looks like they want to knock your head off, you might want to *stop* talking. Maybe even back up and apologize."

Jackson straightened up and faced her, and he surprised Lily almost speechless by grinning at her. She'd seen him sprout nasty, contemptuous smiles before, but never an actual, honest-to-goodness friendly grin, brief though it was.

"I accept the terms of your proposition, Miss Hernandez. I will make an earnest attempt at being . . . *nicer.*"

She grinned back. "Good. And for the last time, call me Lily."

Jackson was about to say something else, but Kaz popped around the corner from the dining room. He had circles under his eyes, and his shoulders looked sort of limp, as if he'd just completed some exhausting feat. "There you two are! Mom and

Dad believe me—finally. They're leaving for my aunt's place in Santa Barbara. So . . . let's get going!"

His face somber again, Jackson nodded. "Yes, we do have a comrade-in-arms in peril, do we not? Let the rescuing commence!"

Kaz stared at Jackson for a few seconds, said, "Okay, whatever," and left the kitchen.

Jackson turned to Lily, his eyebrows and palms raised in bafflement. She put a hand on his shoulder. "Don't worry. He's just confused 'cause you didn't say anything nasty."

As Lily steered Jackson out of the kitchen, he sighed and said, "This is going to take a great deal of work."

A few minutes later, Lily stood with Brett and Jackson in the Smith family's driveway, her hands shoved in her pockets and her line of sight pointedly *not* directed at Kaz and his parents, who stood on the house's front porch, in the middle of a tear-filled good-bye. Beside her, Brett toyed with the Wright family ring, which he'd taken from the pocket of the now-defunct Fake Kaz's hoodie.

Lily already felt pretty rotten that they'd had to drop this bomb on the Smiths and then bail. That rotten feeling got worse when Brett turned to her and said, "We need to get out of here. All of us. Before Kaz starts wavering."

Lily went to Kaz, who had just managed to pull himself out of his mother's embrace. "Kaz, we gotta go."

Kaz looked from his mother to his father and back. "Promise me you'll leave right away. Promise me."

Mr. Smith nodded. "I promise. The girls are already packing."

"I love you both." Kaz turned to Lily, and under his breath, said, "Get me out of here before they guilt me into staying."

Lily said "I'm sorry" to the Smiths and led Kaz down the steps and back to Brett and Jackson. "Brett, do you think you can do that invisible water thing if we're in the air?"

Brett raised his eyebrows. "What, we're gonna fly? I thought you were worried the illusion wouldn't work with the wind?"

Lily reached out to feel the breeze. "The air and I had a talk earlier. I think I understand it better now. And this will be faster than Jackson's disks. No offense, but we need to get to Gabe ASAP."

Jackson shrugged, almost pleasantly. "None taken."

Brett grinned toothily. "Now that's what I'm talking about!" He handed the Wright family ring to Kaz. "Try not to lose it this time, okay, man?"

Kaz stowed the ring safely in his backpack as Brett narrowed his eyes at a sprinkler head. The sprinkler's seal popped, spraying water all over them. Except the water never touched them—instead it curved around them, rapidly solidifying into a spherical version of the cylindrical water curtain Brett had used on them twice before. "I've got it, Lil. Any time you're ready."

Lily concentrated, summoned up a broad cushion of air, and they left the driveway, soaring smoothly upward and away from the Smith family, out of the neighborhood. Kaz's eyes never left his house, even as it dwindled to a tiny speck behind them.

"Thrilled as I am to be plunging headlong through the air again," Jackson said, "I have to ask—Lily, can you maintain this method of travel all the way back to Alcatraz?"

Brett spoke up. "We're not going to Alcatraz."

It was a little challenging to talk and maintain the air platform at the same time—at least it was for her; Brett seemed to be doing his part with no problem—but Lily asked, "What do you mean? The bats took him to the island, didn't they?"

Brett nodded his head in a different direction. "I think that's what we're looking for."

In a detached voice, Kaz said, "Funny . . . I've lived here my whole life, and I've never been there a single time."

Lily finally saw what they were talking about. A glimmering, unmistakable golden halo encircled the top of the Transamerica Pyramid, standing out in stark contrast to the low, angry storm clouds beyond it. Brett said, "That's our target. That where the Dawn is, so that's where Gabe has to be."

Lily swung their course around to head for the massive skyscraper.

"Okay. This is it." Brett turned from the stairwell door and looked each of them in the eye. "Everyone good? Are we ready to do this?" He lingered on Lily. "Sis? You're not worn out?"

Lily shook her head. They'd decided not to use the elevator for fear of alerting the Eternal Dawn that someone was coming, so that had left the stairs. *So many stairs. So. Many.* To keep them from being half dead of exhaustion by the time they reached the top, Lily had carefully guided the flow of air so it not only gave them a boost with each step they took but also supplied them with more oxygen than normal. Consequently, they were about to step out onto the skyscraper's top floor, but they felt as if they'd only taken a brisk walk around the block. "I'm good to go, Brett. Everybody just . . . be careful, okay?"

Brett said, "On three." He counted down, and as he did, the air crackled around them. All their eyes changed. Kaz, his energy restored since the destruction of the apographon, seemed to tremble with power. Anticipation threatened to squeeze Lily's heart right out of her chest. *There could be anything on the other side of that door! Another leviathan! Two leviathans! What are we even doing up here?*

Brett reached "three" and pushed the door open—and a pair of hunters howled and launched themselves through it, jaws cranked open wide, horrible fangs ready to sink into vulnerable flesh.

Lily caught them with a ferocious gust of wind that flipped

them around in midair and drove them like bullets into the opposite wall. The hunters landed with a sickening, crunching smack, and Jackson finished them off with two golden disks that crushed them into the floor.

The four of them piled out of the stairwell and paused. Brett pointed off to their left. "I can hear chanting! This way!"

As they rounded a corner, three members of the Dawn, dressed in full robes and with long, serrated daggers in their hands, rushed out to meet them. Or they tried to. They had taken no more than two steps before Kaz snarled, and the concrete of the floor ripped up through the carpet and clamped around their feet like heavy stone fists.

Brett pulled a column of water out of a pipe—wrecking a small section of the wall to do it—and used the twisting, curling element to smash the weapons out of the Dawn members' hands. Jackson then sent three fist-sized golden spheres rocketing into their jaws, and the cultists crumpled to the floor.

"I'm pretty sure it's about to get bad, guys," Lily said, her eyes on Jackson. "Think you could hook us up with a boost?"

"Done." Shimmering lines of golden radiance reached out from Jackson's body to Lily, Kaz, and Brett, and Lily immediately felt her elemental power grow.

"Come on!" Brett called, apparently abandoning any hope of sneaking up on the Dawn.

As powerful as Lily felt—as powerful as she knew they *all* felt—she didn't really care about losing the element of surprise.

All she wanted to do was rescue Gabe.

And keep the rest of us from getting hurt. Even Jackson. Since their conversation in Kaz's kitchen, she'd felt sort of responsible for him. *We're* all *getting out of this.*

With Brett leading the way, they bounded up a short flight of stairs. Lily saw a small, metallic sign at the base of the stairs that read "Conference Room," with an upward-pointing arrow, and the four of them emerged into a broad, spacious room with floor-to-ceiling windows lining all four walls.

In front of them, silhouetted against the vast, panoramic view of the city below and lit by the circling magick halo above, Primus and about thirty members of the Dawn had Gabe strapped down to a makeshift altar. Gabe's eyes were closed, and his head lolled to one side. Lily heard herself gasp—she'd expected him to be restrained, but he looked really out of it. *We have to get him out of here!* Hunters prowled through the crowd, winding around the cultists' legs and panting.

Poised at the altar, Primus chanted in the Dawn's horrid, buzzing language. She held a slim silver dagger high in her right hand, and in her left, the Emerald Tablet glowed like a lantern.

Lily's power blazed within her, and with a single gust of wind she sent ten Dawn members tumbling feet over head away from the sacrificial ritual.

A cultist screamed, "Stop them! Don't let them interfere!"

The cultists produced knives and guns and charged at them, but five fell immediately when the concrete of the floor surged up and grabbed their legs. One man screamed, and Lily thought she might have heard a shinbone break.

Jackson darted past her, throwing out glowing golden disks and spheres as fast as his hands could move. They cracked against ribs and arms and faces, and five more cultists fell, groaning and clutching the places where the solid-magick projectiles had hammered into them.

But Primus had kept chanting, and now she raised the silver dagger above her head. Lily reached deep into the air, and, with a scream that sounded like the violent wind of a catastrophic thunderstorm, she unleashed a colossal pulse of air upon Primus and the remaining cultists.

It wasn't just that the robed men and women careened into one another, and into the floor, like bowling pins after a strike. Lily had spent the time climbing the stairs learning how to feed extra oxygen into the air. Now she flexed her elemental muscles in the opposite direction and forced almost all the oxygen *away* from the Eternal Dawn.

Let's see how well you can chant without any oxygen, you creeps!

Primus gasped for breath, grabbed at her throat, then dropped the Emerald Tablet and staggered backward. Lily sent fresh, revitalizing air into Gabe's lungs as she sprinted to the altar. Gabe's eyes flickered open, but she could tell at a glance there was something very wrong. "Gabe! Gabe, are you okay? Can you get up?"

She had to put her ear close to his lips to hear his whisper: "Sh . . . shackles . . ." *Of course! Duh!* A pair of gray metal cuffs bound Gabe's wrists to the altar, and as she opened the clasps to free him, odd runes flared to life and died on their surface. Gabe struggled to sit up, and he gave her a grateful smile as she slipped an arm around his shoulders to help him. "Cavalry's . . . what you guys are . . ."

She smiled right back, her legs weak with relief that he was okay. "Come on. Let's get you out of here. I think I can blow out a window and just . . ."

But Lily couldn't finish the word. She couldn't *breathe!* She tried to say, "What's happening?" but the words only came out as bubbles. The world clouded over, blurred and distorted and cold . . .

She turned her head to see Jackson and Kaz to her left. Both of them hovering about a foot off the floor.

Both of them encased in spheres of water.

Brett stood between them, his eyes glowing an intense, deep blue-green and a truly foul grin plastered on his face. His words were distorted as they traveled through the layer of water that encased her, but Lily understood them well enough:

"You're not going anywhere, *mi hermana*."

No.

Primus might as well have stabbed Lily through the heart. It couldn't have hurt any worse.

Oh God, no. Not Brett. Not my brother!

Brett was her rock. They squabbled and fought, but he was someone in her life she knew she could count on, knew she could talk to, knew she could come to if she needed help. Even more than her parents—she could tell Brett *anything*. Brett was the one who'd stood up for her when she got picked on for using her inhaler. He'd been the one who'd talked to her the whole way home from school and promised her everything would be okay. No matter how bad she felt, Brett could always make her laugh.

But now . . .

Was it possible? Jackson had been right the whole time! Brett *had* gotten Gabe captured! Brett had betrayed them. And now . . . was Brett going to kill them?

Is he going to kill me? His own sister? Why?

The enormity of it was too much. Lily felt as if her mind were about to crack in half.

Gabe, the only one of Lily's friends not encased in water, lurched for the Emerald Tablet and snatched it up off the floor.

But with a hideous shriek, Primus threw herself over the altar and drove the silver blade into Gabe's back.

Lily tried to scream. She couldn't.

Gabe staggered, his mouth wide. He didn't make a sound as he crumpled to the floor.

Lily's vision began to darken around the edges. A calm, distant part of her acknowledged the truth: *I am drowning.* Her tears disappeared into the water as she stared, transfixed, at what was happening to Gabe.

She'd seen it before, when the same ritual was performed with Brett, back in the theater: blood flowed from Gabe's wound, but instead of simply falling to the floor, it wrapped around his body, becoming a slick, grotesque cocoon. The blood cocoon engulfed the Emerald Tablet as well, and as it began to consume the book of power, a wave of energy exploded from it. The sight was impossible to process. *It's like . . . shining darkness.* Like the deepest, blackest shadow in the whole of the universe, that somehow blazed with blinding light.

The Tablet shivered once. Twice.

And *imploded.*

The Emerald Tablet imploded as if suddenly sucked into a microscopic black hole, and a blast of force ripped out of the place where it had been like a massive bomb detonating. The shockwave tore into Lily, and while it hurt every square inch of her—*Like being hit by a train*—it also knocked her completely out of Brett's water prison.

Lily slammed to the floor right next to Kaz and Jackson. She was lucky enough to land facing them. She could finally breathe again, but the pain of the blast was so overwhelming that she was afraid she might still pass out.

Where he stood behind Kaz and Jackson, Brett went rigid. His back suddenly arched as if he'd been electrocuted. Lily could see every muscle in his body clenching tight—and at the same time something exploded out of Gabe's blood cocoon like a geyser. Lily watched, her face not five feet from the spectacle, and instead of passing out, now she was sure she was going to throw up.

It looked like . . . like shark chum. Like the scraps a butcher threw out at the end of a day. And it smelled even worse. Gory knots and looping ribbons of blood and flesh pumped out of the blood cocoon, splatting onto the floor, and then Brett actually did vomit.

But what emerged from her brother's mouth had nothing to do with the contents of his stomach. Instead, long, narrow segments of . . . *shadow* fell to the floor. The same kind of impossible shining shadow that had exploded from the Emerald Tablet. Brett bent double, and Lily screamed, because *hands,* hands with too many fingers, hands made of darkness, began to emerge from between Brett's lips and push and pull their way out of him.

"Brett!" She couldn't scream his name loudly enough, her throat raw with fear and horror. *"Brett!"*

Just as the shapeless mass of gut-churning gore had piled out of the blood cocoon, the living, moving mass of darkness finished dragging itself out of Brett Hernandez . . . and as Brett collapsed, his eyes rolling back in his head, that living darkness flowed into the collection of amorphous carnage from the blood cocoon.

The gore trembled, convulsed, and to Lily's utter horror, heaved a great *sigh*. It pulled together, rising up off the floor, a tower of ravaged skin and bone and sinew, and as she watched, unable to look away, it took the shape of a man.

From behind her, Lily heard Primus speak. "Now rejoice in our Founder's return!" she shouted to the other cultists, her voice ringing with pure joy. "Welcome, my lord Thorne," she said, turning to the creature that looked like a man.

"Welcome."

13

Pain lanced through Gabe's back. At first he couldn't even tell what kind of pain it was—burning? Piercing?

"We will always be a family . . ."

The words skittered through his brain.

Mom?

When Gabe finally opened his eyes, he was on his knees, panting, his ears ringing from something. Had there been an explosion?

He looked down and saw the Emerald Tablet clutched in his hands. *Lily! I saw her, and Primus, and . . . Brett . . . there was something wrong with Brett. . . .*

Before the thought could even fully form in his mind, the Tablet crumbled.

He tried to hold the book together, but it did no good. He remembered suddenly that Primus had said the Tablet would be destroyed. But seeing it—this book that they had all risked their lives for time and time again, now turned to a pile of pale golden ash—still felt like a punch to the gut.

Then he noticed the golden ash mingling with some kind of dark liquid on the floor. What was it?

Where am I?

All at once he realized that the liquid the ash had mingled with was blood, and memories of the horrible red cocoon came flooding back. Gabe twisted one arm behind him to explore the place where he remembered the silver knife plunging into his back . . . but felt nothing. No wound at all. *That spot's not even sore.*

Gabe got to his feet. Despite not being able to detect any one source of light, he could see a little. *What's wrong with the air?* Its thin yellow tint reminded him of the light just before dawn, but instead of coming from a sun beneath the eastern horizon, here it seemed to come from *everywhere.* He glanced around, trying to pinpoint the weirdness, and finally realized he was standing in a huge room with a floor and ceiling made of gigantic stone slabs—enormous, rectangular blocks of stone that had to weigh several tons each.

The walls were too far away to see as the yellow-tinged air gradually shifted into gray mist.

No, not yellow. More like . . . gold.

Gabe's stomach dropped out the bottoms of his feet and sank through the flagstones. His disorientation evaporated.

I know where I am.

He crouched and examined the floor more closely. The blood left over from the cocoon, the stone, even his hands—the color was wrong. Not wrong, but definitely different . . . deeper, richer. And everything sort of faded around the edges into a faint golden haze.

Arcadia.

The floor gave a violent shake, almost knocking him down. Something cracked directly above him, and stone dust fell onto his head. Gabe dived out of the way as an enormous chunk of stone collapsed onto the place where he'd just been standing. The impact set off another tremor, and as more stone dust sifted over him, Gabe knew he had to get out of there. Turning in place, he finally spotted a tiny, dim dot of brightness over to his left. *An exit?* He took off running.

A few long seconds later, Gabe passed through a gigantic arched doorway and into a broad corridor. He seemed to be inside some unfathomably huge building. There were no windows; the light he had spotted came from a translucent globe mounted on the wall above head height, swirling golden energy dancing inside it. It took Gabe a moment to realize where he'd seen something like that before.

The theater where Primus sacrificed Uncle Steve. This is just like the "show globe" the Dawn used to transform stray dogs into hunters.

Another tremor shook the floor. He couldn't just stay put, or he'd risk being crushed if the whole place came down on top of him.

Gabe crept along the corridor, hugging the wall. More translucent globes were spaced out along hallway's length. They lent just enough illumination for him to see clearly. The farther Gabe walked, the more recognizable his surroundings became. The hallway opened up onto a balcony, and in the same instant that a familiar scent reached his nose—a scent of salt water and mildew and peeling paint—he got a glimpse of barred cell doors, and it clicked.

This is the Arcadian version of Alcatraz!

Brett had called it a "citadel." Gabe agreed. The word fit.

He moved carefully away from the wall and padded toward the thick railing. For the first time, Gabe got a true sense of the sheer scale of the Arcadian Alcatraz. He stood on the bottom tier of a well the size of a football field, and when he tilted his head and looked up, row after row after row of balconies, all of them lined with cells, stretched up until they vanished from sight. Broad stairways connected one balcony to another. Gabe took a step toward the nearest one—and a sound made him freeze.

He stood perfectly still. Wondering if he'd hear it again. Hoping he wouldn't.

The sound came again. Long, ragged, like air escaping from an ocean cave, dragging itself across barnacle-encrusted rocks.

The sound of *breathing*.

The skin on the back of his neck drew tight. Gabe tried to pinpoint the sound's source, but it seemed as if it were at once everywhere and nowhere. He clung to the railing as he climbed one staircase, and another, and another. He heard more ragged breathing, and something about the noise was terribly wrong. There was a smell now, too: a mix of salt water, mold, and putrid musk like something from a skunk. He coughed and fought to keep from gagging. His eyes watered as he kept on climbing.

On the fifth level, Gabe caught sight of what he hoped might be a way out. Far above him, eight or nine levels up, stood another broad, arched stone doorway, with a show globe mounted on either side of it.

That's got to lead somewhere! And anywhere would be better than here.

Gabe increased his pace. He had just reached the top of the second-to-last staircase when he found two horse-sized creatures waiting for him, their fang-filled mouths widening as they spread out on the balcony to block his progress.

Gabe froze. *Oh God . . . it's a prison! Of course there are guards!*

In one way they were like the hunters and abyssal bats he'd

seen on Earth, with their eyeless, noseless faces and their skin-less limbs dripping with slimy golden goo. But he'd been able to understand the shapes of the hunters and the bats. The bodies of these "prison guards" just . . . didn't compute. He could identify specific features—long, whipping tentacles lined with saw teeth, feet sprouting claws like the tines of a pitchfork—but if he tried to put the whole together, a sharp pain pierced his head and his vision flashed white.

That didn't mean he couldn't tell what they were about to do. They crouched, ready to spring, and Gabe knew he'd have to fight. He'd have to conjure fire from the matter around him, too, the way he had on the leviathan, since there was no electricity in this place. "Come on," he whispered. "Come on, do your worst."

But when Gabe raised his hands and concentrated on the prison guards, willing his connection with fire to come alive, he discovered something else that was different about Arcadia.

Twin streams of white-hot power sprang from his palms like twin lasers. The force of it, the *recoil*, threw Gabe backward, so he almost tripped and fell—but that was nothing compared with the effect the fiery beams had on his targets. They struck the two guards dead-on and burned holes completely through them, and as Gabe watched, stunned, the holes widened until they engulfed the guards' bodies completely, leaving behind nothing but glowing cinders.

For a moment, the Citadel's wet breathing went silent.

Gabe stared at his hands. Summoning fire had been . . . *easy*. No, more than just easy. *Effortless*.

Here, in Arcadia, fire lay all around him, waiting to serve. Eager to leap to his command. In this place, Gabe wasn't going to have to exert his will to bring fire to him.

He was going to have to exert it to hold the fire *back*.

Two more prison guards dropped down from the balcony above and came shrieking toward him. Gabe didn't even lift a finger this time. He merely fixed his burning, roaring gaze on them, and their bodies ignited, turning to ash under the infernal weight of his stare.

Gabe climbed the final stairway. He shrank back when he realized that the cells here were occupied by strange, terribly disfigured prisoners. But then he drew himself up straight. These inmates were monsters, but they were still no threat to Gabe. Not with the fire inside him. Though he couldn't understand whatever language the creatures spoke, he sensed they were *beseeching* him.

Free us . . . help us . . .

His eyes still aflame, the air around him hazy and wavering with the fire's power, Gabe walked past more cell doors, and while he did not help them . . .

Burn, burn, burn . . . the fire whispered in his mind.

. . . he did not incinerate them, either. He could have.

Burn, burn, burn!

But he showed mercy. He was the fire. And the fire chose to

spare these wretches' lives.

BURN, BURN, BURN, BURN . . .

For now.

Gabe made it to the doorway and was about to walk through it and down another long corridor, when a voice behind him spoke.

"Gabriel."

He turned, curious to see who the voice belonged to.

No. That wasn't right. He turned because the voice left him no say in the matter.

"You have delivered yourself to us, Gabriel."

Slowly, slowly, Gabe turned in place, and found himself facing something ten times worse than the prison guards. *How could something so big have moved so quietly?* Like the guards, its rhinoceros-size body was somehow impossible to comprehend—except for its eyes.

Its *human* eyes.

Easily the size of dinner platters, they were blue and shockingly, horrifically human, set above a gaping mouth filled with inward-curving, wickedly pointed teeth. The mouth didn't move as the creature spoke. Its words appeared directly in Gabe's head, written across his brain. And when he realized that this monster, this abomination, must be what was left of one of the original Eternal Dawn members trapped here a century ago, Gabe wanted to claw his brain right out of his skull.

"You won't hurt me, Gabriel," the creature said, and Gabe

knew it was right. *Those eyes.* The fire was still under his control, but . . . he had no desire to do the monster any harm. It crept closer. Its claws made a ghastly clicking sound on the cold stone floor. "Why have you come here, little boy? What is it that you seek? Hmm . . . let me take a look . . ."

It's mocking me. It already knows the truth.

Gabe stood, paralyzed, and as the human-eyed monstrosity began peeling back the layers of his mind, Gabe desperately wanted to scream.

The creature didn't let him.

Gabe could only stand, feeling naked and ashamed and more humiliated than he'd thought possible, as the creature pawed through his mind. Memories, ideas, hopes, fears, desires . . . the creature was paging through Gabe's very essence. And as it did this, it edged ever closer. Inch by glacial inch.

Gabe knew that when the creature reached him, when it had read the Book of Gabe cover to cover, it would kill him and eat him. The hunger oozed from it like a tide of clotting blood. Gabe tried to move his legs, though he knew there was no point.

"Abandoned by your parents." The monstrosity's voice pressed against his mind, a loathsome, mocking violation. "How selfish. And prevented from making any friends by your cruel uncle." *Click, click. Click, click.* "Of course you know, Gabriel, why your parents left you. It's because of how worthless you were. How worthless you still are." *Click, click. Click, click.*

"And your uncle kept you from making friends because you are so relentlessly unpleasant. Spoiled, entitled little brat . . . how could he let any *normal* children associate with you?" *Click, click. Click, click.*

Gabe wanted the voice to stop. Needed the voice to stop.

His mind began to unravel.

Oh God, it's true, it's true . . .

That's why Mom never came back for me. She never wanted me. I'm no good to anybody. I'm nothing . . .

"You are useless. Worse than useless. You are human garbage, little boy." *Click, click. Click, click.*

Please stop. Please, please, please stop.

"You should be grateful to me for seeing you as you truly are. You will serve a greater purpose after all, as I strip the flesh from your bones, bit by bit. I shall start with your feet. So you are *awake* as I eat you. With every bite I tear free and swallow you will thank me for giving your wretched life meaning. I—"

The creature broke off midword. It took a step back, and another, and Gabe saw its wide, human eyes narrow in panic as its limbs grasped at its misshapen throat. As the creature gasped and choked, the sound of a roaring wind filled the tunnel, and a gust of air with the power of a freight train picked the creature up, flung it over the railing, and smashed it down to the floor far below. The abomination's screams echoed through the prison before cutting off with a distant, wet crunch. Gabe realized that he could finally move again, and then Uncle Steve was there in front of him, his eyes blazing silver-white and wet with tears as he crushed Gabe against his chest.

"Gabe. My God." Uncle Steve grabbed Gabe's shoulders and pushed him back to arm's length, his eyes normal again. "Are you hurt? Are you okay?"

It took Gabe a couple of seconds before he realized he could talk—before he realized that the self-loathing the creature had filled his mind with wasn't real. When the words did come, they came in a rush. "Uncle Steve, I'm sorry, I'm so sorry, I've been so *awful*, I didn't understand, I didn't mean—"

Uncle Steve broke off Gabe's words with a single hard shake to his shoulders. *"Are you hurt?"*

Gabe blinked. "I'm, I'm okay, how—"

"Good. Come on! We have to get out of here!" Uncle Steve took hold of Gabe's wrist and hauled him down the corridor, toward the dim but unmistakable outline of a door.

Uncle Steve had two flesh-and-blood legs, Gabe noticed, stunned—but there was no time to ask about it.

When they reached the door, Uncle Steve pushed through it with no hesitation, leading Gabe outside into heavy, golden light. While Uncle Steve shut the door and used air to move large chunks of masonry to barricade it behind them, Gabe tried to make sense of what was ahead of them.

They stood on top of what seemed to be a wide, sturdy wall made of . . . he looked closer . . . *bones*. The bay stretched away in front of him. They had to be at least three hundred feet above the waves, which looked like liquid gold. A grotesque, twisted version of San Francisco squatted on the opposite shore.

Arcadia.

Behind him, Uncle Steve said, "Gabe. There's someone you need to meet."

Gabe turned and saw a tall, slender woman in a billowing green gown standing about thirty feet away, her back to him. Her long, straight black hair flowed and rippled in the wind.

It was the woman from his memories. It was the woman from his dreams.

It was his mother.

14

Lily stared at the devil in black.

Her cheek was pressed to the carpeted floor, her ears ringing and her body aching from the blast. Still, she stared so hard her eyes stung, so hard she wasn't sure if she even had eyelids to close anymore, stared and stared and couldn't stop. It didn't matter that ferocious winds whipped through the room, or that tiny shards of broken glass from the demolished windows lay everywhere. Lily couldn't pull her eyes away from the monster in front of her.

Jonathan Thorne stood head and shoulders taller than the tallest man Lily had ever seen, yet he was so thin that he looked more like a scarecrow than a man. His sallow, gaunt face might have been handsome once, but now it seemed like little more than a framework of bone supporting the two gleaming green orbs of his eyes. He stood before her in a crisp black three-piece suit, like something out of an old-fashioned silent film. Thorne straightened the lapels of his jacket, tilted his head back, and slowly, luxuriously inhaled.

Though like everyone else Primus was still on the floor, reeling in the wake of the explosive ritual, she managed a grateful smile. "It is an honor, Lord Thorne! Welcome to—"

Thorne cut her off with a dismissive wave of one hand. "I know where I am, thank you."

The lights around them began to flicker. In the guttering darkness, Thorne's eyes pierced the shadows with rays of malevolent emerald light. He casually raised his arms above his head and stretched. Lily strangled a gasp. Crimson light shimmered along the lines of Thorne's body as if leaking from the seams.

She was close enough to Brett to tell that he was breathing. This was a relief, but horrible thoughts still chased themselves through her mind. Whatever Thorne was, part of him—part of *it*—had come out of Brett. *That thing was* inside *him! Is he okay?* Lily finally clamped her eyes shut as the full meaning of it sank in.

Oh God, has it been there ever since he got back from Arcadia? Arcadia. Where Primus had just sent Gabe. *What if the same* thing happens to Gabe while he's there? What if something . . . possesses him, like Thorne did Brett?* She didn't want to entertain the other thought creeping around the edges of her mind: *What if Gabe gets killed over there?*

She shoved the idea away. Locked it down tight.

Brett was right in front of her, still on the floor. And looking at him, a ball of ice formed in Lily's stomach. All this time together over the last few days, and it hadn't been Brett at all! With a paralyzing sense of dread, everything clicked into place. The increase in Brett's power. The sudden interest he'd taken in Dr. Conway's research and the Emerald Tablet.

Brett hadn't been himself since returning from Arcadia. He'd been Jonathan Thorne.

Jackson was right all along!

How could Jackson have sensed something was wrong when Lily, Brett's own twin sister, had missed it?

Her brother's head was tilted toward her, so Lily could see how wide and glassy his eyes were. "Brett!" Lily hissed his name. "Brett, can you hear me?"

Brett's head moved a fraction of an inch, and his pupils contracted. "Lily." His voice could barely even be called a whisper.

"Can you move? Are you all right?" She risked a glance back at Thorne, but he had drifted over toward the Eternal Dawn members and seemed to have forgotten about them entirely. *Thank goodness!*

"I'm so sorry, Lil," Brett rasped. "I tried to stop it . . . stop him. But I couldn't. He's so strong. I couldn't. I couldn't."

"Rise," Lily heard Thorne tell the cultists. As the founder of the Eternal Dawn's rumbling words rolled over his followers, the lights dimmed and flickered again. "Rise . . . and attend me."

Lily strained and was finally able to muster the strength to push herself up. *I've got to help Brett! We've all got to get out of here!*

Jackson leaned in close. "Go. Get him to safety. I will provide some cover against the Dawn." He conjured six golden orbs the size of softballs.

Lily followed his gaze to the closest group of cultists. A moment later, the orbs screamed past Lily's head and crashed into the Dawn members like glowing cannonballs. Bones crunched and breath wheezed from emptied lungs, and Lily watched as Jackson got to his feet, his eyes flaring brilliant, fiery gold above gritted teeth.

Kaz pulled Brett up onto his feet alongside Lily. "Come on. We've got to get out of here *right now*." He pointed to a yawning gap twenty feet behind them. "That shock wave knocked a hole in the floor."

Lily nodded, and she and Brett both took wobbly steps toward the ragged hole, but Lily stumbled when Primus's hysterical voice screeched through the air. "Stop those children! *Seize them!*"

The lights flickered again. "Belay that order."

Thorne's voice was still as calm as a lake on a windless day, but it filled the room, echoing until it hammered at Lily's eardrums. But they couldn't let themselves slow. They jumped through the hole to the floor below, and Jackson joined them a moment later.

An elevator stood at the end of a short hallway. Kaz gestured at it with his chin. "There! Come on!"

Lily nodded. She slipped one of Brett's arms over her shoulders, supporting him.

Faintly, from the floor above, the voice of one of the cultists reached them. "But, Master Thorne, shouldn't we capture them? They're attuned to the elements!"

Thorne's voice boomed out as if every surface in the building had become a speaker, broadcasting his words. "The children are irrelevant. Now that I have returned, the city of San Francisco itself will merge the realms with its sacrifice."

Lily froze in place. She whispered, "What'd he just say?"

"Huh?" Kaz asked as he tried to help support Brett from the other side. "Who cares? Let's go!"

Lily slipped Brett's arm free of her shoulders and shook her head. "I need to hear this. You go on—take the elevator and get Brett out of here."

Brett shook his head and looked as if he was going to say something sharp, but when he tried to speak, he staggered and put a hand to his head.

"You heard Thorne. He doesn't care about us," Lily said.

"Gabe was the only one he wanted."

"But—" Kaz sputtered.

"But," Lily continued, "I'll go out a window and float down at the first sign of trouble. I'll be right behind you."

At her side, Jackson surprised her by saying, "*We'll* be right behind you. I want to hear what that monster says as well."

Kaz hesitated, so Lily stepped closer to him and added more urgency to her words. "*Go.* Get Brett someplace safe."

It was obvious Kaz didn't like it, but he got Brett—who was so drained he was literally dragging his feet—into the elevator. Lily waited until the red numbers on the display started counting down before she turned to Jackson. "Come on. We can hear him just fine from here, but maybe we can find someplace to watch him, too."

Jackson fell in beside her. Calmer now that Kaz was getting her twin out of harm's way, Lily could concentrate well enough to summon a cushion of air under her feet. She rose just high enough to peek over the edge of the hole, and didn't know whether to sigh in relief or yelp with fear.

The Dawn members were clustered in front of Jonathan Thorne at the far end of the immense room. She motioned for Jackson to be quiet, and when he nodded, she lifted him up beside her. The two of them watched, peering over the hole's jagged edge, unnoticed.

"The time of the terrestrial elements is at an end," Thorne said. Lily figured he must be getting used to being on Earth now, because the lights only flickered a little bit when he spoke and his voice no longer sounded like it was coming out of a set of stadium amplifiers. A glimmer of gold caught her attention, and she turned to Jackson.

Lily didn't think she'd ever seen two different emotions so clearly displayed on anybody's face before. Jackson Wright was terrified of Jonathan Thorne . . . but he also *hated* the man. The gold radiance glimmering from Jackson's eyes could have been the fires of hell itself.

Thorne went on. "I have come from Arcadia, my loyal children, and I bring with me a new order for this world. A new order for both worlds."

Murmuring broke out among the Dawn members. Lily spotted Primus, standing off to Thorne's right, and she thought the cult leader looked . . . confused. *Yes. Confused and worried.*

Thorne's words might not be magically enhanced anymore, but they still boomed out effortlessly across the crowd. "I have come from the Shadow City, and now this city will pay the toll for the future I have come to deliver. Soon, my children, this vile blue sky shall tear asunder and reveal the true amber and gold behind it. Soon the water shall rise up and take millions in sacrifice. Soon cleansing flames shall billow and roll across the Earth, leaving blackened beauty in their wake. I have come from Arcadia, my children, to see this world undone."

Primus's concern seemed to reach a peak. "M-Master

Thorne? My Lord? Wh—what are you talking about? Are we not going to remake this world into something more glorious? With the magick of Arcadia, the Earth can be brought to a state of eternal dawn, with us as its leaders. Isn't that why our order was founded? Isn't that our purpose?"

Thorne turned his head toward Primus, and her face lit up with the emerald radiance from his eyes. Lily suddenly felt very glad not to be on the receiving end of that stare. Primus recoiled but kept her footing.

"Perhaps," Thorne drawled. "Perhaps, long ago, that was the purpose of the Dawn. But I have returned with but a single desire."

Primus stuttered again but gathered herself enough to speak, "What desire, Master?"

Thorne raised a hand toward her. "Blood."

Lily's mind had a hard time processing what she saw next. At first it looked as though a small part of the world had collapsed in on itself . . . but then, to her own regret, she understood. Part of the shadow essence that had occupied Brett's body leaped out of Thorne's hand and narrowed to a long, thin spike. The spike snapped out like the stinging barb of some ghastly insect, and punched straight through Primus's chest.

The strike took less than a second. Lily blinked, and the long, black shadow-spear had vanished.

Primus simply stood there, staring, as the blood drained

from her face. Lily gasped as another blood cocoon started forming around the woman, streaming from the wound Thorne had made. One of the cultists, a young woman, screamed and rushed to Primus's side, but this blood cocoon was different from the others Lily had seen. This one pushed the young woman's hands away. Sealed her out. The woman collapsed, sobbing, as the cocoon finished forming.

The rest of the cultists backed away from Primus, Thorne, and the young woman. Carefully. Silently.

"He needs no ritual," Jackson whispered in horror. "No silver dagger. No book of power. He can send people to Arcadia at will!"

Lily tensed her muscles, ready to run, because God only knew what kind of Arcadian horror would emerge from the cocoon once Primus had been sent to the other world.

But Jackson took hold of her forearm. "Wait," he hissed. "This isn't the same as the other cocoons we've seen. There's no Exchange. Nothing is happening!" Lily saw that he was right: the blood cocoon wasn't moving. There was no rippling or squirming from anything trying to fight its way out. The cocoon simply finished molding itself around Primus's body and . . . stayed there.

Waiting.

The cultists began murmuring, their muffled words filled with fear, and when Lily saw Thorne's face, she understood why. His pale skin, unnatural green eyes, and jet-black hair *looked* like the features of a human being, but when he grinned his human mask fell away.

Thorne's mouth was filled with triangular, serrated teeth. *Like a shark.* Lily stared, transfixed, and watched as the fangs *changed*, becoming long, needle-sharp spines, like those of some fearsome deep-sea creature—and then changed again, into rings of horrifying, inward-curving hooks.

The horror show that was Jonathan Thorne's grin kept transforming, each iteration more terrifying than the last, and even as Lily struggled to keep herself from running away from sheer terror, she couldn't help but wonder: *What has Jonathan Thorne become?*

Part of that had been inside Brett? *What did it* do *to him?*

"Silence!" Thorne suddenly roared. He pursed his thin lips, concealing his monstrous teeth. "It is true, what you have long been taught. The right elements, the right reagents and words and sacrifice and ritual *can* merge Arcadia with this world. But now that I have come, there is a much simpler way. A way that requires no children playing elementalists." He packed eons' worth of disgust into those last three words. "Listen to me. The corridor between worlds is narrow. Force too many beings through it at once, and its walls will collapse."

One of the cultists in the front row, a tall, tanned woman spoke up with a quavering voice. "But . . . Master Thorne . . . how can we do it? How can we sacrifice so many people at once?"

Thorne flashed his mutant carnivore grin, and Lily had to look away. "The same way Arcadia was created in the first place. An earthquake strong enough to destroy San Francisco. Just as it was destroyed in 1906."

15

The Arcadian wind blew tiny motes of golden light into Gabe's eyes and ruffled his hair. The rest of him remained stock-still, like a statue, as he stared at his mother. She gazed back at him serenely. From behind him, Uncle Steve said something, but the words bounced off Gabe's ears.

Gabe's memories of his mother occupied a space far, far back in his mind, among the earliest thoughts and impressions he could recall. Accessing that space was like dredging up a barely remembered dream. A dream before he could read, before he could speak, before he could even walk without falling down.

Back then, his mother had been his *world*.

Gabe had seen photographs of his mother, and he had connected her face to his memories, but only in an abstract way. To Gabe, his mother was more a collection of sensations. . . . The softness of her skin. The warmth of the blanket she tucked around him in his bed. The blueberry scent of her hair when his face rested on her shoulder. The overwhelming knowledge that, with her, he was safe.

Gabe had felt a heart-stopping jolt that night he'd faced the apographon. Standing there in Argent Court, staring at something that looked exactly like someone so important to him, he'd felt the edges of his world quiver and threaten to buckle.

That was *nothing* compared with what he felt as the woman in the green dress turned and fixed him with her impossibly blue eyes.

"I know you," she said, in a voice like a high note on an out-of-tune piano. "Gabe."

Gabe ran to her and threw his arms around her before he even knew what he was doing. She bent slightly to return the embrace, and with his face pressed to her collarbone, Gabe was transported, thrown back into those flashes of memory from his childhood.

Her skin feels the same! Her hair still smells like blueberries!

He felt the beating of her heart against the side of his face and shuddered to think that he had been fooled by the apographon for even one second.

Gabe loosened his hold on his mother and stepped back.

She straightened up . . . and the euphoric haze shattered. Gabe's throat locked up tight, his mouth instantly dry. His mother looked down at him with her own blue eyes, yes, but . . .

Were her eyes always so big?

Disturbing details sprang out at him like a barrage of punches. Her fingers were long. *Too long.* And he knew she was tall, but he had seen her in photos standing next to his father and Uncle Steve. She'd been shorter than Uncle Steve's six feet, but now, when Steve came to stand next to her, Aria loomed over him by half a head. Plus . . . a few gray hairs threaded their way through his uncle's blond mane, but his mother looked the same age—*exactly* the same age—as she had in the photographs from ten years ago.

Gabe took another step back, the wheels in his head spinning so fast they threatened to come off their axles.

As she regarded him calmly, neither smiling nor frowning, Gabe got the impression that there was something *under* the blue of her eyes . . . something crouched there, waiting, a bare millimeter under the surface.

This is my mother. I know it is.

And yet, in some way Gabe couldn't even begin to define, she *wasn't*.

Something else lived there, inside her. Something dangerous.

The corners of his mother's lips curved upward in a slow, deliberate motion, but the smile didn't reveal her teeth. "You've grown so," she said, but her eyes seemed to focus on the ground right behind him. "The spitting image of your father." Gabe tried to think of something to say, but before he could, she turned away from him and moved closer to the edge of the wall, staring out across the bay at the shadowy city on the opposite shore.

When she moved, Gabe finally noticed a wide swath of . . . *What are those things?* No, more accurate: what *were* those things? On the top of the wall around and behind her lay a scattering of creatures that looked like insects, but each one was at least as big as a small dog, and they had all been *crushed*. Gabe couldn't tell by what exactly, just that they were all very, very dead and leaking their grayish innards onto the bone wall's surface. His mother had been standing at the edge of the insectoid carnage.

Did she do that? How *did she do that?*

Gabe stared at his mother, and as he did, black and gold shadows rose and swirled around her like a terrifying cloak.

Gabe couldn't take his eyes off her as he grabbed his uncle's wrist and led him what he hoped was far enough away to be out of earshot. Uncle Steve didn't seem surprised, and he dipped his head to make it easier for Gabe to speak to him in a whisper.

"That's—that's my *mom*."

Uncle Steve nodded. "Yes."

Gabe let go of his wrist but moved closer. "What *happened* to her?"

Uncle Steve's face was creased with pain. "Arcadia happened to her. The place itself. Magick is poison, Gabe. Spend too much time with it, and it leaves a mark. And if *you're* here . . . that means Jonathan Thorne is in San Francisco. Plotting to spread magick's poison across the entire world."

Gabe put up protesting hands. "Forget about Thorne. That's my *mom*!" He pointed to the woman cloaked in shadows. "How do we get her back to San Francisco? If she's sick with magick stuff, how do we . . ." He tore his gaze away from his mother and looked his uncle in the eye. "How do we make her *better*?"

The pain on Uncle Steve's face grew deeper. "Gabe . . . there's no way to send her back. Maybe if we'd gotten to her years ago. But she's been in Arcadia too long. She just . . . she doesn't belong on Earth anymore."

Gabe shook his head. "No. *No.* Okay? She's just sick. There's gotta be a—a ritual or something! To get the magick out of her! There's rituals for every other freaking thing; there's gotta be one for this!"

Uncle Steve let out a long, ragged breath. "There isn't. I'm sorry. If she went back, she'd spread magick's corruption with her, just like Thorne. I hate to say this, and I wish more than anything that it weren't true, but the only world where you and Aria can be together is this one."

For a long moment it felt as if Gabe couldn't breathe.

It's not fair. It's not fair!

He wanted to scream the words. Or just scream. He turned his back on his uncle, and the tears welling up in his eyes hissed into steam as the fire rose inside him.

Gabe hadn't let himself hope. Not truly. When Brett had told him his mother was still alive, even when he saw the apographon, deep in his heart, Gabe hadn't dared let himself hope. It was too much to wish for. Too much to be real.

But she *was* alive! She was standing *right there*. He could've hoped! He could've pinned all his dreams on this, and it still wouldn't have been enough to save her.

"I tried everything to get her back before—before it was too late." Uncle Steve spoke over Gabe's shoulder, and when Gabe realized the quaver in Steve's voice came from his own welling tears, it shocked the fire back into place. "I tried everything." Gabe had never heard this tone in his uncle's voice before. "I swear to God. I tried everything to get her back." Gabe realized Uncle Steve was asking for his forgiveness.

"We should leave this place," Aria called, still gazing out across the water. Her clear voice carried extremely well, but its off-key, warped-bell quality made Gabe's skin crawl. Immediately, he felt guilty.

Mom, what happened to you?

"Come on." Uncle Steve beckoned for Gabe to follow him as he went to join Aria. "She's right. We have a safe place, and once we get there, we can figure out how to get you back to Earth. Let's go."

Gabe stood between Aria and Uncle Steve and watched as Steve's eyes turned silver-white, just like Lily's did when she commanded the air. "Relax," his uncle said. "I won't drop you." Gabe's stomach lurched as his feet left the wall, and a pillar of air sent him and his mother and his uncle sailing out across the waters of the bay.

Gabe stared down, so far down, at the water, a shimmering gold instead of the blue-gray of the real world. The black, twisted spires and broken streets of Arcadia loomed ahead of them, and the gold-and-amber sky swirled overhead.

Magick. Everything is saturated with magick. No wonder the fire wants to run wild here!

The closer they got to the city, the more awful it looked. Gabe saw creatures, tiny at this distance but unmistakable, winging through the air and scrambling over buildings and shattered roads. The city was a nightmare come to life.

But nightmare or not—for the first time in ten years, he was with his mother and his uncle. Yeah, his uncle had grown back a leg that had been missing for a solid decade, and his mom had become some sort of magick-soaked monster, but nobody's perfect.

"I don't want you to worry, Gabe," Uncle Steve told him. "We *are* going to get you home. I don't know how, but we'll come up with something."

Home. Without a family, what did the word even mean? But thinking of San Francisco made Gabe remember how he'd been sent to Arcadia in the first place.

"I meant to tell you—the Emerald Tablet's gone! The ritual the Dawn used to bring me here, it turned the Tablet to dust in the process."

"The Book of Power destroyed!" Uncle Steve exclaimed. He couldn't have looked more shocked. "It was thousands of years old! The foundation text of all our magickal knowledge!" he sputtered. "It was written by . . ." He trailed off. "Well, I guess it doesn't matter now. But the Tablet created Arcadia. Without it, I don't how Arcadia can ever be destroyed."

"Everything casts a shadow," Aria said unexpectedly. Gabe thought he'd never get used to the strange dissonant key of her voice. "This world is the darkest of shadows," she continued. "The darkest of reflections."

Gabe expected her to go on. When she didn't, Gabe looked at Uncle Steve in hope of some explanation. But Steve seemed to be just as confused as Gabe was. Then it clicked.

Wait. What was the first thing she said? "Everything casts a shadow"?

"Hold on. I overheard something else before I got sent here!"

"What do you mean?"

"What Mom said about casting shadows—Primus said it, too! After the Dawn grabbed me, I heard her talking about another book like the Emerald Tablet. She called it . . ." Gabe struggled to remember. "The Mirror Book? It's the Emerald

Tablet's shadow or something."

Uncle Steve's face winched itself even deeper into a frown.

"The Emerald Tablet doesn't cast a shadow," Uncle Steve muttered to himself. Then Gabe saw his face light up. "Correction! The Emerald Tablet doesn't cast a shadow *on Earth*."

"So you think that—"

"Another Book of Power!" Uncle Steve said excitedly. "Here in Arcadia. A shadow of the Tablet, just like this dimension is a shadow of our own."

"That's why Primus wasn't all freaked out that she had to destroy the Tablet in the sacrifice!" Gabe said, now just as excited as Uncle Steve. "Because somewhere there's another book that can do the same thing!"

"The Mirror Book," Aria said dreamily.

Both Gabe and Uncle Steve peered over at her, startled.

"Yes," she said airily, "I know where that is."

Uncle Steve had set their small party down a few hundred feet from the water's edge. Now they made their way along the city's buckled sidewalks, following Aria. Gabe kept his eyes on the ruined houses that lined the boulevard. That way he didn't have to look so much at the dead horses littering the broken street, half-concealed by mounds of rubble.

It had taken Gabe a couple of minutes to realize that, while he and Uncle Steve shuffled along the street, Aria just sort of . . . *glided*. Her long green dress hid her feet, but Gabe was pretty sure they were hovering a couple of inches off the demolished roadway.

His mother also hadn't said a word since they'd descended to street level. She just started walking—gliding—without even a glance over her shoulder. Gabe and Uncle Steve had no choice but to follow along.

Her silence was unnerving, but so were the streets that they walked. In much the same way he chose not to look at the dead horses, Gabe let his eyes slide past the alleyway draped to the rooftops with thick, white spiderwebs. He also skirted carefully around the hole in the street from which he could hear a buzzing like thousands upon thousands of beating wasp wings.

Staying quiet and doing his best not to draw any attention to himself might actually be a very good idea.

After trekking a dozen blocks, Gabe spotted something slimy and golden moving in the shadow of a half-collapsed house. When the creature emerged, Gabe immediately recognized the lean, skinless features of a hunter. Striding nimbly over a mound of shattered masonry, it looked as at home in the ruined city as a lion on the savanna.

Like the hunters Gabe had seen in San Francisco, this creature had no eyes. But that didn't stop Gabe from shivering when the beast turned directly toward him.

The hunter's muscles coiled and tensed as it prepared to charge.

Gabe called up balls of fire around his hands. The hunter

leaped up on top of a low brick wall, opened its fang-filled jaws wide . . . and froze.

Gabe thought it *sniffed*.

Aria hadn't slowed down as the hunter emerged from hiding. Gabe didn't think she even saw the monster, or if she did, she didn't care. She just kept gliding along the sidewalk, and the closer she got, the more the hunter trembled. Finally, with a long, low, mournful bay, the hunter whipped around and bolted in the opposite direction.

Gabe turned to his uncle and spoke very quietly. "Did you see that?"

Steve nodded grimly but didn't say anything.

Gabe watched his mother as she led the way. An emotion he never, ever would have expected to associate with her suddenly presented itself, and it was impossible to ignore.

Fear.

The fear only intensified when he saw a flock of ten abyssal bats come diving toward them, only to bank sharply at the last second and climb, shrieking, back into the sky.

It went on like that for what felt like ages as they made their way deeper and deeper in the shadow city. Aria silent, Gabe worried, and Uncle Steve, as far as Gabe could tell, pensive. Aria turned and led them down a cobblestone street toward the bay—*away*, to Gabe's relief, from another pair of houses draped in thick, white spiderweb—and Uncle Steve finally broke the silence. "I think I know where we're going."

Gabe was grateful to focus on something other than his mom and his worries about whatever she had become. "Yeah? Where?"

Steve pointed off to one side of the street, his arm angling toward the water. "Black Point. I believe that's what it's called. She's taking us to Fort Mason . . . or whatever version of Fort Mason they've got here."

Gabe had seen Fort Mason before, from a distance, riding in the car through the city. He knew it was a bunch of low, red-tiled buildings . . . but when Aria led them around the corner and he got an unobstructed view of the place, Gabe sighed. "Of course."

Arcadia's Fort Mason was a massive mission-style palace, with arcades hundreds of feet high. What was unassuming red tile on Earth was here some kind of red-gold gem-like substance, and Gabe had to shield his eyes when light from the Arcadian sky glinted off it. An entry portal—he couldn't call this gigantic thing a mere door—stood at least thirty feet tall, and Gabe gasped when he caught sight of the two biggest hunters he'd ever seen standing guard in front of it.

"Uh . . . are they going to run away, too, when Mom gets close?"

Uncle Steve squinted. "I don't think those two will be running anywhere."

Gabe immediately saw what he meant. The two "guardian" hunters weren't covered in gold ichor. They actually *were* gold. A pair of ornamental statues. He was more relieved than embarrassed for mistaking them for the real thing.

"Come along, Gabe," Aria said. "We're almost there." She looked back at Gabe, and though she didn't smile, there was a welcome twinkle in her eye. Frightening or not, she was his mother, and he quickened his pace to walk beside her.

"It kind of looks like a library," Gabe said.

"A good place to find a book, I guess," Uncle Steve said.

"Right, but it looks deserted. I was expecting . . . I don't know. A fortress. Like, with guards and defenses and stuff? If the Mirror Book's so valuable, why isn't the Dawn protecting it?"

"The Dawn doesn't dare enter this place," Aria said as the shadow of the library palace fell across them. She raised her eyes to the towering walls and didn't say anything more.

Gabe huffed. "Why be afraid of a library? Books can't hurt you!"

For the first time, as she turned to face him, Aria smiled fully. Her lips stretched, and stretched, and stretched, until a horrid, Cheshire-cat grin split her face in half, literally reaching from ear to ear. But that wasn't the worst of it. The mouth that had once kissed him and sung him lullabies was filled with far, far too many teeth. And every one of them came to a needle-sharp point.

Gabe looked at her in horror and then realized he'd been wrong.

The Emerald Tablet had been used to create Arcadia. It had gotten his dad killed and trapped Gabe in another dimension. It had delivered a demonic monster to San Francisco and turned his mom into . . .

Gabe took a deep breath, turned to the library, and prepared himself for anything.

A book had started all this trouble in the first place.

16

Brett moved one foot in front of the other, testing the strength of his legs.

His legs, he had to remind himself as he walked.

After days of being a prisoner in his own body, each step seemed like its own miracle.

He felt split down the middle. Half of him relished the familiar sights and sounds and smells of San Francisco. The other half of him still held on to foul echoes of Thorne. He struggled with the knowledge that he'd been worn like a suit, a vehicle for something so horrifying that his mind could only glance at it before having to turn away.

Being possessed by Thorne had been like being a hostage in

a vehicle driven by a madman. And there had been times when Brett had felt blindfolded, unable to tell what Thorne was up to, as the monster walked in his sneakers and spoke with his voice.

But Brett had seen enough to know that Thorne had conspired with Primus to arrange the ambush in Greta's room at Brookhaven. He knew that Thorne had sabotaged the water glyphs at Argent Court to broadcast its location to the Dawn.

Perhaps worst of all, he knew that Thorne had nearly drowned Gabe in order to allow the Dawn to capture him.

While sharing the same body as Thorne, Brett had touched the surface of the man's dark heart. He'd felt the apocalyptic hunger of the beast's desire. He'd glimpsed a century's worth of horrific acts he could not—and did not want to—comprehend.

And always one particular image flashed brighter than all the others, hovering there at the edges of his perception. Something red. Circular. *Reptilian?* He could still see it.

Brett tried to focus on it, but it slithered away.

"Where *are* they?" Kaz's hands fluttered. They both stood by the entrance of the Transamerica building. "What if Thorne's got them? What if he's putting that shadow goop in them now?" Kaz seemed to realize what he'd just said, and his fluttering hands got even flutterier. "Oh, Brett! I'm sorry, I didn't mean, I wasn't trying to—"

Brett was going to tell Kaz not to worry about it, but just then a gust of wind blew his hair back, and Lily and Jackson dropped straight out of the sky and landed right in front of them.

Lily's silver-white eyes faded to dark brown as she threw her arms around him. He hugged her back, and they stood like that for a long while.

"Hermano," she eventually whispered into his neck. "Are you okay?"

"I'm okay," he said. He wanted this to be true, but he was afraid to let go of her. He was afraid of what he'd done while he was Thorne's puppet and terrified of what would happen next.

She drew away from him and stared into his eyes for a long moment, then spoke gently. "I really want to get you out of here."

He wanted that, too, but first he had to ask. "Gabe?"

Lily's jaw clenched. She shook her head, her eyes glistening. "They . . . they exchanged him. Traded him for . . . the rest of Thorne. Gabe must be in Arcadia now."

Brett drew breath to speak, but he stopped when what sounded like distant thunder rumbled. He looked skyward to the Transamerica building's crowning pyramid.

He was horrified to see waves of golden light rippling from where the building pierced the sky. Concentric waves of magick were coursing outward from the tower like ripples on the surface of a pond.

Lily's eyes flickered, brown to silver to brown, as she stared up at the display. "It's Thorne. Jackson and I heard him say he's planning to use another huge earthquake to merge Earth and Arcadia!"

Kaz said, "What? *How?*"

"Let's just say we don't want to be here when it gets started," Lily said. "We need to go."

"Sounds like a good plan to me," Brett said.

"I concur," Jackson agreed.

For the first time, Brett took a good look at the smaller boy. It was only a moment before he had to look away. The sight of Jackson in the flesh reminded Brett of his own mistakes—mistakes that had led them into the terrible danger they were up to their necks in.

"I don't think it's safe to fly with so many abyssal bats around, but if you'll stick close, I can speed us along," Lily said.

They started walking quickly. Winds flowed around Brett, gently supporting him, providing extra lift along the backs of his legs and under his feet. As Lily led the way, Brett couldn't help admiring her control. Assisted by her air, they were walking in fast, long strides with hardly any effort. Within moments they were blocks away.

Lily led them into a little park studded with cypress trees. When they stopped, Lily fixed Brett with serious eyes. "Before we go any farther, are you *really* okay, *hermano*? Are you, y'know . . . *you?*"

Brett slumped against a concrete wall. He couldn't blame

her for asking. "I'm me. Yeah. All that . . . that other stuff. *Him.* It's all gone now."

"We're really glad you're back, Brett," Kaz said. "But what the heck do we do now?"

"We've got to get Gabe back," Lily said.

"And we must also stop Thorne from manifesting a disaster of the magnitude of the 1906 earthquake," Jackson said.

"Right," Kaz said. "Okay, not to be a pest or anything, *but how?*"

Lily cleared her throat. "Brett, since you sort of had Thorne *in* you, can you think of anything that might help?"

Brett frowned. This was the last thing he wanted to think about, but he had no choice. His best friend's life might depend upon it. Not to mention the lives of everyone else on the planet. "The last thing I really remember, I was in Arcadia, down in the bottom of this *massively* screwed-up version of Alcatraz. And I was staring into these huge green eyes."

Kaz shuddered. "Thorne has green eyes. Just like Gabe." He seemed to realize what he'd just said, and his words tumbled over each other. "Not that there's anything wrong with having green eyes! I'm not saying Gabe's like Thorne! Except, I guess he's Thorne's descendant? But that doesn't mean he's *like* Thorne!" Lily put a hand on Kaz's shoulder, and he fell silent.

Brett went on. "It *was* Thorne. I realize that now. But it was like . . . his eyes were *huge.* They looked human, but they were also, like, the size of freaking Volvos. And the rest of him, it—" With a shudder, he remembered the enormous mass of tentacles writhing inside a thundercloud. "He isn't human anymore. I don't think there's a word for whatever he is now."

Lily took his hand gently. "And that's it? There's nothing else? You woke up a few minutes ago?"

Brett sighed. "I can remember bits and pieces. Like how a dream comes back to you sometimes." He let go of Lily's hand and covered his face. He didn't want to remember, but more than that: trying to remember *hurt*. Like the memories themselves were laced with barbed wire. "Ugh . . . Thorne was . . . it was like he was *reading* me. Digging through me, looking at all my memories all my thoughts . . . learning about the world. The *modern* world. He even learned how to sound exactly like me. God, I can still feel him in there!" Brett thumped one fist against the side of his head. For a heartbeat, he saw a flash of *red. Circular . . . Scales.* He took a breath, and the image vanished. "It's like he left a slime trail through my whole brain."

Kaz said, "Ew."

Lily shot Kaz a look. Kaz blushed and stared at his feet.

Brett glanced back and forth between his sister and Kaz and steeled himself. "Guys, I need to tell you something."

After everything that had happened, Brett had decided something. Thorne had done terrible things while inhabiting Brett's body . . . but Brett was no saint himself. And it was time his friends knew the truth.

Brett opened his mouth, but for a moment, no words came. Finally he forced them out. "Thisisallmyfault," he said, rushing through the words. "All of it, from the very beginning. I'm the one who contacted Ghost Dork over there . . ."

Jackson stood up straight. "I beg your pardon!"

But Brett plowed onward. It was hard enough to start telling Lily and Kaz what he'd done. If he let Jackson stop him, he wasn't sure he'd ever finish his confession. " . . . and got this whole mess started, and then I *really* screwed up and let Thorne in. But it was only because . . . because I was trying to find Charlie, and Jackson told me that—"

Jackson said, "Look here, now is not the time to—"

Lily put up a hand to shush Jackson, and asked, "What did Jackson tell you?"

Brett continued. Slowly. Haltingly. "He promised me . . . he said, 'Death isn't the end. Dead isn't *gone*.' He swore to me that Charlie was in Arcadia. That's why I did all this. The ritual that bound us to the elements down in the tunnels. Getting Gabe to unlock the Emerald Tablet. I was following Jackson's instructions every step of the way."

By the time Brett was finished, Kaz was glaring at Jackson, but Lily couldn't seem to look at him. She turned her back on all of them, her eyes shut tight.

Jackson puffed out his chest, as much as he could with his thin little frame, and his mouth twisted into his trademark sneer. But then he stopped. Midbreath, he turned away, hunched his shoulders, and mumbled something at the ground.

"What was that?" Lily spun toward him. "What did you say?"

Jackson didn't turn back around, but he spoke over his shoulder. "I said I'm sorry. I should not have lied to you, Brett. I just . . . I was *trapped*, and scared, and lonely." His voice broke with pain. "I wanted to get out. I *had* to get out."

Harsh words bunched up in Brett's mouth. He wanted to scream at Jackson, curse him, threaten him, make him feel every bit as bad about what he'd put Brett through as Brett did himself. But just as quickly as the anger appeared, Brett felt it ebb and fade away. Because how long had Brett been trapped, used as Thorne's shell? How desperately had he wanted to escape? What would he have done to be free?

Jackson was trapped, too. He was trapped for over a century.

Brett realized he and Jackson had been—what did his grandmother say? *Two peas in a pod.* Just alike. Both of them craving something that seemed impossible. Both of them willing to do whatever it took to get it.

"Look. We both made some serious mistakes. Lily, I did this to find Charlie, but . . ." It was the first time Brett had let himself really think about this in a long while. "The thing is, Lil . . ." Tears spilled down his cheeks. "I think he's really gone. I think Charlie's gone for good." He knew he couldn't stop the tears, and he didn't try. There was a time when he'd have been furious to show such weakness. He would have yelled and shoved to keep people from seeing it. Tonight he didn't care. As tears filled Lily's own eyes, Brett said, "Charlie's dead. He's really dead. Dead and gone. And there's nothing anybody can do to bring him back."

Lily's glistening eyes ran over. Her lower lip trembled. She shook her head, shook it again, swallowed hard . . . and sank down onto the pavement, sobbing. Her arms wrapped around her knees. Her face hidden, Lily cried, and every time her body shook it felt like a blade to Brett's heart.

He knelt beside her and slowly put his arms around her. Lily's arms unwound from around her legs, and she raised her tear-streaked face to his and hugged him.

"I'm so sorry, Lil," he breathed. "I'm so sorry."

Lightning flashed overhead as dark clouds billowed and rolled. With a brittle crack of thunder, the sky opened up and wept along with them.

Lily's words hitched and wavered through her tears. "I miss him. Every single day." She hid her face against his shoulder. "He was supposed to teach me to drive! He was supposed to show me how to play guitar! We had . . . *plans*." The sobs came back full strength, and she didn't try to talk anymore.

Brett felt that blade to the heart plunge in deeper. All this time, Lily had been hurting every bit as much as he had. But she'd been so focused on making sure *he* was okay, he'd never given much thought to how *she* felt. She had always been so positive, so supportive. So *good*.

"Think how much we can do with our elements, Brett. I can make us fly! We can battle these terrifying creatures! We can combine *worlds*. We have so much power! But no matter what we do, Charlie . . . Charlie's still gone. And now Gabe's gone, too."

Brett didn't say anything else. But he thought that maybe Lily didn't need him to. She just needed her brother to hold her.

Brett lifted Lily's face with a finger under her chin. "It's okay, *mi hermana*." With the corner of his sleeve he wiped away her tears. "It's gonna be okay. *We're* gonna be okay."

Lily nodded. She even tried for an unstable little smile.

I don't deserve her. I don't deserve any of my friends.

Overhead, the rain slowed and stopped, and a breeze blew the dark clouds apart.

All of this was his fault. Brett knew it. But maybe . . . *maybe* . . . there was a way to fix some of it.

Without warning, the strange image flared again. This time, it hit him like a blow between the eyes. He staggered and would have fallen, but one of Lily's wind gusts buoyed him up. He got a better look at it this time: *a red snake.*

It didn't make any sense, but he couldn't shake it, and when he squeezed his eyes shut it only made it worse. *Red snake. Red snake. Red snake.*

"I remember something from when Thorne was inside me! But I don't know what it means!"

On his other side, Kaz asked. "What is it? Something from Arcadia?"

Brett shook his head violently, both to answer no and to try to dislodge the image. "It's a snake! A red snake!" He pulled at his hair in frustration. "I can't stop seeing it!"

Brett opened his eyes in time to catch Lily and Kaz exchanging baffled glances. Kaz said, "Do you remember where you saw it? Or what was around it?"

Brett didn't have time to consider the question.

Sudden thunder like a cannon shot left Brett's ears ringing, and all four of them slammed into the ground as a tremendous quake shook the earth. A terrible crunching sound crashed out from a nearby building, and they dashed out into the street in time to see several tons of concrete and steel collapse.

"Come on!" Lily shouted. Her tears were gone, and her eyes flashed silver-white. Wind swirled around them. "We need to get away from the buildings. We're not far from the harbor!"

Brett wondered if he could ever be as truly strong as Lily was.

As they ran up the street, debris smashed into parked cars on either side of them and trees bucked and uprooted. The pavement fifty yards in front of them buckled, snapped, and threw a moving car completely off the road and into a storefront.

"Come on!" Brett shouted, or tried to shout. He still felt so weak. "We should see if those people need help!"

Lily poured on the wind speed, and the four of them

reached the car. It had turned upside down, its rear end lodged into a display of designer dresses, and Brett started to say, "Get the doors open!"

But he stopped short.

Even without crouching down to peer through the windows, he recognized the blood cocoons. The car had held four passengers. Four blood cocoons now rested inside the cabin. Pulsing. Waiting.

Brett was still staring when Lily came to his side, and said, "Oh *no*."

"How is this possible?" Brett asked. "How can they be sent to Arcadia from a car accident?"

Jackson's ordinarily solemn face turned scarily grim. "I am afraid this is what Thorne intends. This is the purpose of the earthquake. Everyone who would have died in the disaster will become encased like this. Sacrifices waiting to happen. Waiting to be triggered."

Lily nodded vigorously and gestured at the car. "He did this to Primus, too. Put her in a cocoon like this."

Brett stared at the blood cocoons in the car. "So he puts everybody in San Francisco in cocoons and then, what— sacrifices them all at once?"

Kaz squeaked. It wasn't even verbal.

Lily nodded. "He said it'd be like 1906 again! Thousands and thousands—*tens of thousands* of people are gonna die, and he'll send them all to Arcadia at the same time!"

"Give me a lever and a place to stand." Kaz's voice had gone very quiet.

Brett said, "What?"

"Archimedes, the Greek mathematician. He said something like, 'give me a lever and a place to stand, and I'll move the world.' The earthquake. It's Thorne's lever. Except he's not going to move the world, he's going to pry open the doors to another one." Kaz's eyes flickered from dark brown to slate gray and back. "In the usual exchange ritual, one person on Earth gets switched out for someone else in Arcadia. But ten thousand sacrifices? A hundred thousand? All at once? It'll knock the walls down. Guys, we can't let him do this."

Lily said, "Brett—what about *Abuela*!"

"I know," Brett said. If the city was destroyed, their grandmother would be right in the middle of the disaster zone. "We have to stop him. We *have* to." Brett threw his head back and turned in a small circle. "But *how?* How are we supposed to do that, with Gabe stuck in Arcadia and no Emerald Tablet?"

Jackson's eyes flared brilliant gold, and all three of them turned to him.

The thin, pale boy said, "I have an idea."

17

Gabe felt sweat bead across his forehead as Aria grasped the library's monstrous circular door handle. The door looked as if it weighed at least a ton. A low, awful grating sound rolled out from it as Aria dragged it open, but she didn't seem to be exerting any real effort. Gabe wondered how strong she really was.

Aria's blue eyes gleamed as she turned to him and Uncle Steve. "In you go now."

Gabe frowned, and Uncle Steve spoke up. "Aren't you coming with us?"

Aria gave them only the ghost of a pointy-toothed smile as she stepped to one side and gestured them into the building.

Gabe swallowed hard. "I guess it's just us."

Uncle Steve peered into the gloom. All Gabe could see was a long hallway lined with doors. The air itself was infused with dim light, but not enough to keep the hallway from fading into shadows. Gabe couldn't get a sense of how deep the corridor went. "Stick close to me," Uncle Steve said. "I don't want to hear any *Scooby-Doo* 'let's split up' nonsense."

Gabe nodded. "Not even close to a problem."

Slowly, constantly peering around for anything strange, Gabe and his uncle walked into the library. Aria shut the door behind them.

Moving as quietly as he could, Gabe went to the first of the doorways along the hall and peered around its frame. He got ready to jerk back if anything sprang at him from inside—but he was relieved to see that the room was free of monsters. Just walls lined with shelves, every shelf packed tightly with books.

The room smelled of dust and old paper and bookbinding glue. And even in the midst of a sinister palace library in a shadow city on another plane of existence, he took a smidgen of comfort from that.

Libraries smell like libraries no matter where they are, I guess.

He went to the next doorway, and the one after that, and found much the same thing. Bookshelves abounded, crammed with volumes of all sizes, shapes, and colors. An endless series of rooms opened off empty hallways. Each room, Gabe figured, was about twenty feet by thirty, rectangular, and every square inch of every one of the rooms' walls was covered in bookshelves.

The hallway stretched out in front of them and faded into darkness. Maybe it *was* endless. Gabe figured that in Arcadia, anything was possible.

"It's so quiet," Gabe said. "I mean, I know a library's supposed to be quiet, but not like this. Do you feel like we're being watched?"

Uncle Steve said, "Yes, everything about this place is unnerving. We have to be careful. We'll take it room by room. If the Mirror Book is here, we've got to find it."

Going to different shelves, Gabe and Uncle Steve began to pick through the array of tomes. *The Short Life of a Lost Boy in a Dark City. Apologies to a Dead Mentor. The Unyielding Temptation of Flame.* The books Gabe found were all titled in English, and—Gabe couldn't help noticing—appeared to be on subjects just a little too close to his own situation. *The Hungry Fire. On Accepting the Loss of a Mother.*

The pit in his stomach seemed to deepen with each spine he read. Every book here could have been written about him. He sidled closer to Steve and saw his uncle's face was pale and lips grim.

"Uh, the books here, they're like—" Gabe began, but he didn't need to finish the sentence.

"Yes," Uncle Steve said. "For me, too. The library—or whatever this place truly is—seems to be reflecting elements of ourselves back at us. The titles represent our fears or hopes or history. It's insidious."

"So if this place can look inside us," Gabe said. "That means that it knows what we want."

"Worse than that. It means it knows how to stop us from getting it," Uncle Steve said.

Gabe was about ask something else when he caught a flicker of movement from the corner of his eye, near the doorway. Except when he turned to look, there was nothing there.

"Did you see that?"

Uncle Steve turned quickly. "What?"

"I thought I saw something. Over there." He pointed.

Steve crossed the room cautiously and peered around the doorframe. "No, I didn't see anything. And there's nothing out in the hallway now."

Gabe shrugged, frowning. "I might be seeing things."

"In a place like this? You're almost certainly *not* 'seeing things.' Just stay alert. Let's move on."

As they stepped out into the hallway, Gabe stopped Uncle Steve with a hand on his arm. Reading the titles of those books, seeing his worries and regrets engraved into leather, had made Gabe think of all the things he wished he could change. And here, in a shadow dimension straight out of a nightmare, he didn't know how many chances he'd have to put things right. "Listen, I want to tell you that I'm . . . I'm sorry."

Steve paused. "Sorry for what?"

"For acting like such a little snot. For yelling at you back before this all started. For not understanding. All those years, all the moving around . . . I know you were trying to keep me safe. I mean, it still sucked. But I get it now. I just wanted to tell you, I appreciate it, and, uh . . . I love you."

Uncle Steve took a long moment before finally pulling Gabe into a sideways, one-armed hug. "I love you too, kid. And it feels great to hear you say that. I know it wasn't easy on you. All the moving. All the secrets. But you're a good kid, Gabe. Always were. And twelve-year-olds are *supposed* to act like little snots. Right?"

Gabe grinned. "So . . . like, what are you *like* when you don't have to worry about killer magickal doomsday cults all the time? You ever, y'know, chill? Do something fun?"

A smile played around Uncle Steve's lips. "I don't know that I can even remember what I was like. Not have to worry? Have fun? What language are you even speaking?" His face took on a thoughtful expression, though mischief still lingered around his eyes. "I do think I used to have fewer gray hairs, though. I'm almost sure of it."

In that moment—the first truly honest, unguarded moment he could ever remember having with his uncle—Gabe realized how lucky he was. How lucky he'd always been.

He was trying to think of something to say when Uncle Steve's head snapped up, peering down the hallway. Gabe tried to follow his line of sight. "What? What is it?"

"Like you said. Thought I saw something."

Gabe stared down the hallway, but it looked utterly deserted. He couldn't even see motes of dust moving in the air. Uncle Steve said, "Come on, let's get to the next room." Gabe followed him. As far as he could tell, they were utterly alone, but that didn't stop all the hairs on the back of his neck from standing straight up.

They moved on to the second room, which looked just like the first. Gabe approached the nearest shelf. The first book was called *Skylines of Doom and Shadow.*

"Wait," he said.

"What? What's wrong?"

Gabe pointed at the title. "This book. It's . . . I'm pretty sure was in the first room, too." He scanned the nearby spines, and all their titles were familiar. "All of these. I've already seen them."

Uncle Steve glanced at the shelf nearest him. "You're right. Let's try the next room," he said.

But they found the same thing in that room, and in the room after that, and the one after that, too.

In the fifth room, Uncle Steve scowled and muttered a word he had made Gabe promise never to say in polite society. "Of course. Of *course.*" He turned back to Gabe. "The books are arranged differently, but . . . all these rooms. They're the *same.* The *Mirror* Book. Just like the book titles reflect elements from ourselves, each of these rooms are reflections of one another.

This is both a mind game and a maze of illusions. A Library of Mirrors."

Gabe slumped. "So if the Mirror Book isn't in any of the ones we've already been through . . . that means it's just plain not here at all?"

Uncle Steve opened his mouth but stopped when a voice floated toward them from out in the hallway. A voice that crackled and hissed.

"Ga-a-abe . . . come here, Gabe . . ."

He and Uncle Steve stared at each other, wide-eyed.

Uncle Steve said, "Stay behind me," and went to the door. Gabe followed closely—closely enough to peer under his uncle's arm and get a good look at what waited for them outside in the corridor.

A boy stood there. He was on fire.

Gabe choked back a frightened cry.

The boy had Gabe's face. No, more than that—it *was* Gabe. Same clothes, same hair, but flames licked up and down his limbs, his torso. The boy's flesh blackened, cracked, bubbled, but immediately re-formed itself, burning and healing, burning and healing. He said, "*There* you are," and smiled, and Gabe wanted to scream.

"It's a fire elemental," Uncle Steve said quietly. "Fire come to life."

"What does it want?"

The elemental laughed. It sounded like tiny explosions.

"You're smart enough to know, Gabe." It raised its hands, and the flames around them flared white-hot. "I want you to *burn*!"

The elemental thrust its hands forward, and Gabe shoved Uncle Steve out of the way. He felt his eyes burst into red-orange infernos. Twin lances of fire shot out from the elemental's hands, but Gabe took control of them, bent them to his will, so they crooked ninety degrees and scoured the ceiling above.

The elemental grinned hugely. "Yes! Good! More, more, *more*!"

Gabe could hear Uncle Steve shouting behind him, but he couldn't afford to pay attention. The fire elemental curled its fingers into claws and lifted them above its head, and columns of flame burst up from the floor around Gabe like bars of a cage. The books in the room behind him caught fire, and Gabe saw the ceiling was burning, too. The cage of columns began to close in on him. Gabe knew they would consume him if he didn't stop them.

But he could stop them. He *would* stop them. Because the fire belonged to Gabe, not this elemental creature. Gabe knew the fire. *He was the fire.*

Gabe gritted his teeth, and the cage-bars scattered away from him, dancing across the floor, leaving blackened troughs in their wake before they puffed out. He took a great breath and *screamed* at the elemental. A vast gout of fire bellowed from his mouth like the roar of a dragon. As the flames washed over the fire elemental, it took a staggering step backward. Gabe was dimly aware that more and more of the library had started burning around him.

The elemental regained its balance, its grin spreading wider. "Yes, Gabe! Let it burn. Burn. *Burn. BURN.*"

Horrified, Gabe realized he recognized that voice. It was the one he had heard in his head. The all-consuming, rage-filled presence that wanted him to give in to the destruction, give in to the fury, abandon any thought of control, and lay waste to the entire world. *This was that voice.* All his fire-borne rage given form.

Gabe's skin suddenly felt very hot. His eyebrows and eyelashes blackened and turned to ash. Blisters raised on the tips of his fingers.

The fire elemental wanted Gabe's rage to consume the world, but if he couldn't stop it, that same rage would burn Gabe along with it.

A vast sucking sound overtook the hallway, and Gabe fell and slammed into the floor. Starved of oxygen, the fires guttered out in the blink of an eye. Gabe lifted his head just in time to see a fist of wind snatch the fire elemental off the floor and fling it, screaming, so far down the hallway that it disappeared from sight.

Uncle Steve carefully picked Gabe up off the floor. At first Gabe couldn't breathe because the impact had knocked all the air out of him. All he could do was cling to his uncle and croak out, "Thank you . . ." *He saved me. Saved my life. Again!*

Then Uncle Steve's eyes shone silvery-white, and air flowed back into Gabe's lungs. He sucked it in gratefully.

"Are you all right?"

Gabe looked at his blistered hands. "It burned me. The fire burned *me*. I didn't . . . I thought that couldn't happen."

Uncle Steve glanced around. "Now this place is reflecting our own elements back at us. Turning them against us. Come on, we've got to get out of here."

"But what about the Mirror Book?"

"We can't use the Mirror Book if we're dead." Uncle Steve took Gabe's elbow and led him hurriedly back down the hallway toward the massive entrance doors . . . but in front of them, the corridor stretched out. Dark. Endless.

Uncle Steve stopped. "Oh. Sorry. Wrong way."

They turned around, and in front of them . . . the corridor stretched away into the darkness. It was like a pair of mirrors set to reflect off each other into darkest infinity.

We're trapped!

Then a low, breathy voice laughed from somewhere in the shadows.

Gabe moved closer to his uncle. "What's going on?"

A breeze ruffled Gabe's hair. It felt as if someone were running fingers across his scalp, and he winced and tried to brush it away. Uncle Steve groaned. "I'd guess now it's my turn."

"Your turn indeed, Steven." The low voice spoke from the

nearest doorway, and they both spun toward it. Standing there, leaning against the frame with his arms crossed, was a man who could have been Uncle Steve's twin . . . except that, around the edges of his body, he simply *faded away*. It hurt Gabe's eyes to look at him for more than a second at a time.

Gabe took a firmer hold on his uncle's arm. "So that's . . . an air elemental?"

Uncle Steve nodded. "First one I've ever seen."

"And the last." The air elemental didn't move, but its eyes turned a hard, metallic silver, and Gabe's breath choked off in his throat. Suffocated, just like Uncle Steve had snuffed out the fire elemental's flames. It only lasted for a second, but when he could breathe again, Uncle Steve was gone.

Between one heartbeat and the next, he just disappeared. So did the air elemental. Both had vanished, as if they had never existed.

"Uncle Steve?" No one answered him. Gabe suddenly felt very small and very alone. "Uncle Steve!"

Faintly, from some impossible distance down the corridor, he heard his uncle's voice, shouting. *Screaming*, though Gabe couldn't tell whether in anger or pain. He took off at a sprint, heading toward the screams, and almost ran headlong into the wall of flames that sprang up directly in front of him.

"Feed the fire," the elemental said from a few paces behind him, and Gabe whirled to face it. Its voice had taken on a hissing, sibilant quality, like a gas leak in the moments before a catastrophic explosion. "You know you want to. You've never been good at anything but dessstruction."

"That's not true," Gabe said. But as the words left his mouth, the events of the last few days came back to him, and he had to wonder.

His eyes ablaze, Gabe seized control of the flame curtain behind him, compressed it into a ball of fire the size of his head, and threw it straight at the elemental's face. Laughing, the elemental dodged to one side—moving like fire itself, dancing, flickering—and the fireball crashed into the floor behind it and dissipated.

Books burst into flames all around Gabe. Fire crept up the walls. He knew the entire place would burn down if he didn't stop it.

"Ssstop it?" the elemental hissed, reading Gabe's mind. "You do not *want* to ssstop it. All the anger you have felt, your entire life. All the powerlesssnesss . . . all of that isss gone, Gabriel. You have power now. You *are* power. You are fire. Now feed it. *Die for it.*"

The elemental darted forward and clamped its hands down on Gabe's forearms. It felt as if Gabe had thrust his arms into an incinerator. His skin blistered, started to crack—and time slowed down. Gabe could see *through* the elemental's hands. He could watch the damage being done to him.

But suddenly it didn't hurt anymore.

Suddenly the burns felt like cool, clear spring water.

"Yesss. You undersssstand now, Gabriel. You want thisss. You *need* thisss."

And Gabe *did* want it. He wanted his whole body to burn . . . because that would free him, wouldn't it? There would be no more pain, or fear, or worry. Everyone would understand, once he was nothing more than a pile of ash and charred bone. Everyone would see his anger. They would feel it. They would know the same burning pain that had lived in his heart for so long. He imagined people standing around the scorched remains of his body, his mind's eye flitting from face to face, taking in the sympathy there, the sadness, the regret, the—

Lily.

Lily would be there.

And Brett and Kaz. Mom and Uncle Steve, too. Even Jackson.

They'd all be mourning his . . . his death?

Something shifted in Gabe's mind. In his heart. In his *soul.*

Time sped back up to normal, and the fire elemental's grin vanished. Gabe twisted his arms, broke the elemental's grip, and slammed his own hands onto the elemental's shoulders.

"Nice try," he gritted out. "You almost had me."

The elemental seemed to realize what was about to happen. Its cruel, funhouse-mirror version of Gabe's face softened. "Gabe, don't. Don't! I'm you! Can't you see that?"

"You're the growl in my stomach," Gabe said, his voice low and terrible, like the hissing flow of red-hot magma. "You're a hangnail." His grip tightened, and the elemental's body flickered. Parts of it darkened. Disappeared. "You are the fire. *You are what I control.*"

"No . . . pleassse . . ."

"And I'm putting you *out.*"

The elemental shrieked—and for a second, less than a second, Gabe found himself staring into a different face. A face Gabe had carved deep into his memory. Then it burst into a shower of sparks and faded away.

Gabe stood there, in the middle of the burning library. Almost absently, he waved his hands, and the fires around him winked out.

Why had the fire elemental, in its last instant of existence, worn the face of the burning man from his dream? Just before it had vanished, why had it stared at him with the face of his own father?

Gabe shook his discomfort out of his head. He had to focus on finding Uncle Steve.

He was about to call out for his uncle when an earsplitting noise like a million panes of glass shattering crashed all around him. Gabe shut his eyes and clamped his hands to his ears—too late.

The sound faded.

Gingerly, Gabe opened his eyes.

The library was gone. Where its shelves had been, nothing remained but shards of faintly golden glass. Uncle Steve had been right. This entire place had been like a funhouse illusion. A Library of Mirrors. The small room where Gabe now stood was empty except for a single volume, floating in the center of the sparkling debris. It was cloaked in shimmering blackness, and Gabe knew it had to be the Mirror Book.

The black haze around it evaporated as soon as Gabe touched it. The Book, clad in reflective silver instead of its counterpart's emerald, fell into his hand. It was cool against his blistered fingers. Clutching the Mirror Book to his chest, he pushed through the room's only door.

Outside, Uncle Steve lay in the middle of the hallway—which now had no other doorways, no other rooms opening off it—gasping for breath. Gabe ran to him and knelt beside him. "Uncle Steve! Are you okay? What happened?"

Steve's eyes turned silver-white, and his breathing quickly evened out. Shakily he sat up, rubbing his throat, and looked around with a confused expression. "The air . . . I couldn't tell . . . couldn't tell what was real. It was all just an illusion . . ." His eyes finally settled on Gabe. "Is that really you? Are you real? *Are you real?*"

"I'm real, Uncle Steve. It's me. It's Gabe. And look what I found." He waggled the Mirror Book.

Uncle Steve's eyebrows shot up. "Oh, thank God that

wasn't all for nothing." Gabe helped him to his feet. "I think we should get out of here."

Gabe couldn't have agreed more. They hurried as fast as they could to the huge entrance door and, with a helping hand from a channeled stream of air, heaved the enormous portal open.

Gabe knew something had gone very, very wrong as soon as they walked outside. The amber-gold sky, unsettling enough in its own right, had turned an angry bloodred. Above the soaring center spire of Alcatraz Citadel, scarlet clouds churned like stormy ocean waters.

Gabe didn't even have to ask his uncle what it meant. He knew.

Something was happening in San Francisco.

Something really, truly, deeply bad.

18

Lily, Brett, Kaz, and Jackson skimmed down Mason Street, heading for the waterfront. They had to get to Alcatraz, and the breach, so they could try to communicate with Gabe. But first they had to get out of the chaos of the quake-rocked city.

No strangers to earthquakes, the people of San Francisco had dealt with the first event by staying calm and following emergency instructions. But then the first quake had been followed by two even more serious tremors.

It was now clear that this was not a run-of-the-mill earthquake. The idea that this might be the beginning of "the big one" seemed to have registered to the people of the city, and their panic had begun to intensify. By now many streets had buckled and cracked so badly that travel by car had become impossible. So people ran, shouting, in throngs through the city.

Lily still didn't want to draw undue attention to herself and her friends by actually flying, but she'd put even more strength behind the tailwind that lent them extra speed as they ran. They now zipped along as fast as if they were on bicycles. With some experimenting, she'd grown fairly comfortable bending the air around them so they could hear one another speak at normal volume, too, and now Brett ran right next to her, his face grim as he listened to Jackson outline his idea for destroying Arcadia.

"Look," Jackson said. "If Greta Jaeger was right—and so far, we have no reason to think she was not—there is a chance that we can perform the ritual to completion and destroy Arcadia, using Gabe's participation *from the other side of the breach*."

Lily's stomach churned as they passed more and more blood cocoons on the street, all of them victims of Thorne's earthquakes. When he'd claimed enough victims, Thorne would send them all to Arcadia at the same time. And then . . .

Then the walls come tumbling down.

To their left, a house shook and split almost down the middle, and a second later a plume of flame shot up through the wreckage as the gas line broke and ignited. The smell of concrete dust and smoke was everywhere. The shock waves from

Thorne's magickal earthquake were getting worse and growing closer and closer together.

"Kaz, have you still got all the stuff we need?" Lily said. "Jackson's family ring and whatever?"

"I still harbor grave doubts about using the ring," Jackson grumbled.

Kaz ignored him. "I've got everything, yeah. We don't have the Emerald Tablet, but Gabe was holding it when he was sent to Arcadia, so all we can do is hope he still has it. But, guys, even with all the right ingredients or reagents or whatever, how are we going to pull this off? It took me two whole days to learn how to make one little earthquake, and even then I barely kept it from shaking a hospital to pieces. Now we're supposed to destroy an entire *reality*, with zero time to practice? What if we mess it up? What if I forget the words? What if one of us has a panic attack and throws up all over the components? Not . . . not that anyone would do that. Okay, I might do that. Guys, I'm probably going to do that."

"That's not what I'm most worried about," Brett said. He still looked really pale around his eyes and mouth. Lily could only guess how physically drained he was, but she had a good idea of the toll his ordeal had taken on him emotionally. He'd survived Thorne and Arcadia, but the secrets he'd kept from Lily and their friends must have been just as heavy a burden. She hoped that coming clean about them had helped at least a little.

"What is it, Brett?" she asked.

"Gabe!" Brett blurted out. "We can't destroy Arcadia with him in it. We just *can't*."

Lily glanced at Kaz, who nodded. Jackson took a few long moments but finally agreed. "No, I suppose we cannot."

Lily nudged the flow of wind around them to help steer clear of a multicar pileup thick with blood cocoons. Another wave of tectonic thunder rumbled all around them. "There has to be something we can do. Everyone think."

Kaz frowned, pulled his backpack off, and scrounged inside it. After a couple of seconds he pulled out what looked like two cracked ceramic bowls. "Could we use this?"

Brett's eyebrows rose toward his hairline. "What the heck is that?"

Kaz slung his backpack back over his shoulders, took one bowl-like object in each hand, and deftly fitted them together. In an instant Lily realized what Kaz held: the disembodied head of the apographon. She just barely kept from squealing. "Kaz! Why in the world are you still carrying that creepy thing around with you?"

He looked sort of sheepish. "I didn't want to just leave it with my family. But listen, people who get sacrificed during the right ritual are swapped with somebody who's in Arcadia now, right? But only if they're part of the same bloodline—if they're not, it just ends up bringing over some giant crazy monster, like when it happened to Brett." He took a deep breath. "So . . . do you guys think, maybe, if we got the apographon to turn into Gabe's mom again, we could swap it for him? I mean, if it's got a little bit of her life energy in it still. We could try to send it through and get him back?"

Jackson seemed to chew that over. "It is an intriguing hypothesis, Kazuo. It may be worth an attempt."

Lily tried to look at what Kaz was saying from every angle. The problem was, she didn't feel as if she could *see* every angle. *So much of this stuff goes right over my head. But if Kaz and Jackson think it could work, I guess we should try.* But then a thought occurred to her. "Hold on. If that were possible, why didn't Greta and Dr. Conway try it before?"

"Well, maybe they did?" Kaz said. "But now that the breach is open, things might work that didn't before . . ."

"That's an awful lot of 'ifs' and 'maybes.'" Lily cleared her throat. "And even if it works, that still leaves Dr. Conway and Gabe's mom. What do we do about them?"

Kaz looked crestfallen. Jackson stared straight ahead, his eyes narrowed and his mouth a thin, hard line.

Lily glanced at Brett. A crease had formed between his eyebrows—which she knew meant he was in some kind of pain. His lips were moving, too. She hoped he might have an idea. Maybe some weird but useful occult knowledge of Thorne's had lodged somewhere in his brain. But when she leaned toward him to hear, she just heard him whispering, "Red snake . . .

red snake . . . red snake . . ." Over and over and over, his eyes unfocused.

It gutted her to think about it, but Lily had to wonder if Brett's entire mind had made it back from Arcadia. Or how much of it might have been . . . *eaten* by that horrible shadow sludge. How much of her twin was left?

"Brett." She wasn't sure what to ask. "Is there . . . some way I can help with this 'red snake' thing?"

Brett groaned. It sounded half angry, half embarrassed. Then he turned his face away and shook his head.

Lily was grateful to see the water's edge coming up in front of them. As they slowed to a stop, Lily said, "Okay, who's driving?"

Jackson stepped forward. "It would be my pleasure." He turned to look at Lily and the others. "But that means offense will be your collective responsibility." He pointed across the bay to the sinister haze of bats that clouded the silhouette of Alcatraz in the distance.

Kaz had put the apographon head back in his pack. His eyes flickered and went solid slate gray, and a cloud of rocks and gravel lifted off the ground and started orbiting protectively around him. Lily thought it looked like Saturn's rings. Kaz said, "I'm ready."

Brett's eyes had gone deep blue-green, and he stared out across the water with a focus and a . . . Lily had to call it a *hunger.* She raised one hand and made half a dozen tiny whirl-winds dance around her palm. "I'd say we're as ready as we're going to get, Jackson."

Jackson nodded. His eyes snapped from pale blue to brilliant, metallic gold in an instant, and a broad golden disk with upturned edges materialized in front of them. "I believe the railroad parlance is 'all aboard.'"

No one spoke as the golden disk glided across the bay, hovering two feet above the wave tops. Brett hadn't volunteered to conjure a camouflage curtain. Lily didn't even know if he could anymore. *Thorne was the one who did that, not Brett.* But she guessed it didn't matter. The ongoing shock waves were giving the residents of San Francisco a lot more to care about than four kids on a weird-looking shiny raft.

The rocky outline of Alcatraz grew larger and larger as they approached, and the dark haze visible from the shore resolved into what it actually was: the thousands of abyssal bats that had been flocking around the island for days now.

As Lily watched, a group of bats broke away from the island and winged their way toward the golden disk, shrieking and baring their loathsome fangs. "Who wants to take them out?" She was expecting Brett to cause waterspouts to spring up and drown the creatures or something, but instead green light flickered around Kaz's gray eyes as he sent his cloud of rocks and gravel blasting toward the bats like the discharge of a gigantic shotgun.

Lily was pretty sure the flock never even knew what hit it. One second they were flying, and the next they had become a golden mist and a few tumbling tufts of gooey fur.

The rocks and gravel dipped into the water, washed themselves clean of abyssal bat gunk, and returned to orbit around Kaz again, below his well-earned look of self-satisfaction. Lily grinned at him with renewed respect.

"Well done, but there's no time to celebrate," Jackson said. With a nod of his head, he gestured behind them.

Lily turned to see what Jackson was referring to and saw that a much larger mass of bats had broken from the main swarm and were screaming toward them twice as fast as the last batch. But now Brett's eyes shone with ocean-deep blues and greens, and columns of water rose up from the bay's surface like . . .

Like the leviathan's tentacles.

One after another, the watery appendages reached into the air to grasp at bats and drag them down. Brett's lips drew back from his teeth in a snarl as the surface of the bay picked the sky clean. As the last of the ichor-covered flying marauders disappeared beneath the waves, Jackson's golden disk rose from the water and deposited them on the Alcatraz dock.

With his ammunition stones still circling him, Kaz raised his eyes toward the island's peak. "Lily? We might need you for this."

Lily followed Kaz's line of sight, and a cold ball of fear

formed in the pit of her stomach. So far they had faced maybe a hundred abyssal bats, but thousands of them still shrieked and whirled through the air above and ahead of them. Maybe *tens* of thousands. All of them hovering between them and the breach.

Blocking them from rescuing Gabe.

The icy ball of fear flashed hot. *Boiling* hot.

"You might want to stand back," Lily said.

Above them, the already overcast sky had begun to churn, and the clouds above Alcatraz turned sooty black. Lily raised her arms, her fingers splayed wide. The darkness overhead twisted. Became a slowly revolving cylinder of black, cyclonic power.

The abyssal bats didn't seem to know what to do against such power. They wheeled and circled, confused.

A funnel cloud so huge that it looked like an upside-down mountain emerged directly above the center of the island. Silver-white lightning crackled out of Lily's eyes—the boys yelped and jumped out of the way as bolts flashed out and scorched the dock—and with a prolonged scream that boomed like thunder, Lily clenched her hands into fists and brought her arms crashing down.

The funnel cloud slammed out of the sky like the fist of an angry god. Everywhere the abyssal bats flew, the funnels from the super-tornado followed, snatched them up, and whipped them about like the tiniest scraps of brittle autumn leaves.

Like the air, for a moment Lily was everywhere. She carried the rain that lashed across everyone on the docks. She was the bolts of lightning that arced out of a thunderhead to spear the dock in front of her. She was the gusts of wind that crashed like cannonballs into the leathery bodies of her enemies.

Finally Lily's thunderous scream died away. The power, the fury of the cyclone whirled inside her, and she spoke in a voice she didn't entirely recognize.

"What fools send winged creatures against air itself?"

The voice was all wrong. It wasn't her. It was pure power. Pure, cold, sharp, merciless power.

Lily *hoped* it wasn't really her.

Then, like the burst of a sudden gust of wind, the alien fury faded and left her. Without it, she collapsed to her knees, and the soot-black funnel cloud dissipated overhead.

She felt suddenly exhausted. She listed sideways, but Brett caught her.

"Lil! Are you okay?"

Gabe was trapped in another dimension. Their city was crumbling, and their world was about to be undone. But for the first time, Lily felt certain that she and her friends could fix all of it.

They *would* fix it. Because they *had* to.

"I will be," she told Brett.

Kaz came to stand beside them, Jackson right behind him. Kaz said, "Okay, first off, Lily, that was *freaking amazing*. But second, I think if we're going to get to the breach, we'd better do it now."

Lily got to her feet. "Any more bats?"

Jackson's eyes flickered a brief gold, and she realized he was smiling. It still looked so *weird* on his face. "I see not a single abyssal bat in the sky, my lady."

Kaz chuckled. "No kidding. You cleaned *house*."

Brett gave her a proud, respectful grin. "My sister the badass."

Lily brushed herself off and led them off the dock. "Great. Then let's do this."

19

Gabe scanned the top of the Citadel's towering bone wall as Uncle Steve brought them in for a landing, but there was no sign of the insect-like creatures from before. Even the carcasses his mom had squashed were gone.

As they'd flown across the bay, Gabe had thought, *I can't believe we have to go back to the Citadel.* It felt like going back into the belly of the beast. But he guessed no place in Arcadia was truly *safe*—and Uncle Steve had the idea that if they could get to the breach, they might be able to figure out what was happening back in San Francisco. Gabe couldn't argue. He hadn't noticed the Arcadian side of the breach when he'd arrived in Alcatraz Citadel, but he hadn't exactly been in the mood for sightseeing. It had to be there.

He had a fireball ready to go as they opened the enormous doors, but no guards waited inside for them, just as no bug monsters had peered out of gaps in the bone wall. *Wonder if that's because Mom's with us?* He glanced back at Aria, gliding behind them. The three of them moved silently down the long hallways to the gargantuan plunge of the Citadel's hollow center. Still nothing confronted them . . . but he couldn't help letting out a long, soft whistle at what he did see.

The cells were all empty. Every door had been mangled, twisted, and torn from its frame.

In a hushed voice, Gabe asked, "What do you think happened here?"

To his right, Uncle Steve stepped up to the railing and looked down, then far, far up. "I hesitate to guess. But it was nothing good. We can be sure of that much."

Gabe had never before so intensely experienced the feeling of being watched. "Where did they all *go*?"

Uncle Steve shook his head, wordless. Gabe looked over his shoulder again at Aria. She'd fallen silent back at the library, when she'd first laid eyes on the Mirror Book. She hadn't said a single word on the trek back here, and now she just stood, her hand lingering over a bit of twisted metal as she examined one of the ruined cell doors.

Gabe sighed. "Okay. Well. The breach has to be here somewhere."

"If it's where you say it is in our world, back on the real Alcatraz Island, it should be."

The logic made sense, but Gabe could also somehow *feel* the breach's presence nearby, just as he could back in San Francisco. Thinking of San Francisco made Gabe wish his friends were here. A wave of unexpected, acute homesickness made him want to curl up on the floor.

Next to him, Uncle Steve leaned back out over the railing and looked down at the floor of the well. "It's not down there." He raised his head. "I thought I felt something strange last time we were here, and now that I'm looking for it . . ." He pointed skyward, to the top of the hollow tower of the Citadel's center spire.

Gabe tried to follow his uncle's example, and reached out with his elemental senses, the same way he did when he was looking for invisible fire runes. *I do feel something from up there! Way, way up there.*

He glanced at the stone steps that corkscrewed up into the hazy distance.

He gave his uncle a pained expression. "That's a lot of stairs. How many, do you think? Thousands? Millions? We're going to have to climb an infinite number of stairs."

Uncle Steve conjured up a grin. "Not quite infinite. We'll feel the breach, the closer we get to it. And as for the stairs, I think you're forgetting"—his eyes flickered silver-white, and he rose a couple of feet off the floor, currents of air lifting his hair around his head—"the benefits of being an elementalist."

Gabe matched his uncle's grin. He turned to Aria. "Hey, Mom? Can you help us look for the breach?"

Aria pivoted where she stood. Gabe was almost positive that she didn't actually move her feet to do it. A dreamy expression occupied her face, and it took her two or three seconds to focus on Gabe, but when she finally did, she said, "Oh, yes. Of course. Lead the way."

They fell into a pattern. Taking the terraces three at a time, Uncle Steve used the air to levitate them, and when they touched down they made a circuit of the balcony, all of their elemental senses on high alert for the energy emanating from the breach.

Gabe knew, just *knew*, that some horrendous, clawed, tentacular insect monster was going to jump out at them at any second. He kept imagining that he heard breathing, or the sound of some grotesque armored limb clicking against the cold stone floor. Every shadow cast by the gold-flickering globes mounted to the walls could be something waiting to ambush them.

Gabe made himself feel a little better by summoning his own illumination: a hovering orb of fire the size of a baseball that floated above his outstretched right palm. But that only led to a different kind of anxiety, since his connection to the fire was so much stronger and . . . well, *easier* here than on Earth. He worried that if he lost his concentration, the fire orb might explode and set them all aflame. It was impossible not to think of the fire elemental he'd fought in the Library of Mirrors. That had been the incarnation of the inferno that lived inside him. Gabe shuddered when he remembered its endless hunger to rage, and destroy, and *burn*.

Almost better to just look around in the half-dark.

Almost.

They had just touched down on the . . . Gabe realized he'd lost count of how many levels they had climbed. Fifty? Sixty? He couldn't see the base of the spire at all anymore, and he didn't want to think about what would happen if something distracted Uncle Steve in the middle of a levitation. He thought about suggesting they switch to the stairs . . . but then he noticed his mother standing perfectly still, an odd look on her face.

That was really saying something, considering how odd she usually looked. She had her face tilted up and her head cocked to one side. As if she'd heard something, or seen something in the distance.

Gabe said, "You okay, Mom?"

Then an impact like a battering ram hit him squarely in the back and knocked him sliding across the floor.

Gabe slipped over the edge of the balcony and fell.

He screamed as he plunged. His mind raced, desperately spinning in a frenzy of possibilities: *Maybe I can blast myself to safety. Maybe I can melt the floor. Maybe I can fly like the Human Torch does. Maybe I—*

Gabe's right arm suddenly felt as if it was about to be ripped off his body, and his thoughts stopped short. He had just slammed into the railing of a balcony below, and he scrambled madly to get a grip on it, his breathing short and sharp and sliding past panic into hysteria.

From somewhere far above he heard Uncle Steve's voice, distant and small. *"Gabe? Gabe!"*

Groaning, Gabe slid between the bars of the railing and sprawled onto the balcony floor, wheezing and marveling at how much his arm and his shoulder and his ribs hurt. *If that had happened on Earth, it* would *have torn my arm off.* He could still feel his arm, but try as he might—and he tried really, really hard—he couldn't move it.

Gabe hitched himself a foot or two away from the edge and was about to get to his feet . . . when an enormous, terrible weight came down on his left foot, pinning it to the floor like a bug to an entomologist's display board. Gabe wrenched around, trying to get a look at what had trapped him even as he tried to struggle free.

Two blue eyes—two *human* eyes—the size of saucepans stared back at him, set over a wide, grinning mouth filled with familiar backward-curving fangs. The rest of the creature's body was coiled behind it, a mammoth mass of shadowy muscle and sinew.

"No." Gabe could barely get the word out. "You died. You fell! I saw you fall. You *died.*"

Just as before, the creature didn't speak with its mouth. Its words seared directly into Gabe's mind. "You saw what I wanted you to see, little elementalist. You think you understand this place? You think you understand *death*? You do not. But I shall teach you."

Gabe raised a hand, and red-orange flames sprang to life around it, but the creature's voice immediately boomed out inside Gabe's skull. "No. You will use none of your power. You will not resist me in any way. Not this time." The creature stepped forward. One of its claws raked down Gabe's thigh, leaving a painful ribbon of blood behind it. "This time I am ready for you."

The air stirred around them. No—the air stirred, whistling and then roaring, and Uncle Steve stepped over the railing behind the monster. "Thought you would've learned from last time," he said, and his silver-white eyes crackled with electricity as a hurricane blast lifted the creature's body off the floor.

"Learn I did!" the creature bellowed.

Gabe gasped as he watched the creature's limbs *stretch*, stretch and sink enormous claws into the stone and metal of the balcony, anchoring it in place. The vile blue eyes narrowed as they focused on Uncle Steve.

"You will stop that nonsense at once," it said, and Gabe made a tiny, hopeless sound as Uncle Steve dropped his arms to his sides, his eyes fading to normal. Gabe could tell the creature was now looking deep into Uncle Steve's mind. The wind died away as if it had never been there at all. The creature dropped back to all fours. "Come here, little man. Little master of the air."

Gabe could see that Uncle Steve didn't want to do it, but slowly, agonizingly, he put one foot in front of the other, dragging himself forward until he stood right in front of the creature. Casually, as if swatting a fly, it reached out with one colossal forelimb and knocked Uncle Steve to the floor, face-first. Gabe cried out as a small pool of blood began to form underneath his uncle's head.

The creature swung its huge, inhuman head back to Gabe, and long ropes of its saliva fell across Gabe's legs. "Now that that distraction is out of the way, I promised you in our last encounter, Gabriel, that I would take my time with you. But look where that got me." It picked Gabe up off the floor by his neck. Gabe struggled to breathe, but the telepathic monstrosity wouldn't let him move his arms. "I believe now that the best course of action will be to end your life without further delay."

Its fang-filled, gaping mouth opened even wider. It pulled Gabe closer, turning him to position his head directly beneath its slime-covered fangs.

A strange calm overcame him. *I'm with my family. I'm not alone.* He knew there were worse ways to die.

Gabe closed his eyes.

And a voice said calmly, "Get away from my son."

Abruptly Gabe could move again. The creature dropped

him, and he scuttled away from it on his hands and his heels. The creature's blue eyes had widened in—Gabe couldn't believe it—*fear.*

"No," it said. "You mustn't. Begone from here."

Aria glided toward it, passing right by Uncle Steve. All of her terrifying focus was on the creature. As Gabe stared, Aria's skin turned completely translucent, and her eyes grew even larger, and her snarl revealed every one of her long, pointed teeth, and she screamed, *"GET AWAY FROM MY SON!"*

The creature detonated.

That was the only way Gabe could describe it.

The force of Aria's words struck it, and it *exploded* like some kind of demented firework. One second there was a revolting creature the size of a bus, and the next there was a cloud of golden mist, shot through with tiny, swirling black motes. A few seconds more and there was nothing at all.

Gabe stayed sprawled on the floor, looking up at his astonishing, impossible mother, until Uncle Steve groaned and rolled over onto his back.

Aria watched Gabe impassively. She had gone back to what passed for normal. For the hundredth time, Gabe wondered what exactly his mom had become. He wanted to hug her and run in terror at the same time.

He pulled his gaze away, scrambled to his feet, and ran to his uncle.

"Uncle Steve! Are you okay?"

Both of Uncle Steve's eyes had blackened, and blood poured down over his upper lip. "It broke my nose," he said, his words a little mangled. Steve felt the tip of his nose very gingerly, squeezed his eyes shut, and with a sharp motion snapped something back into place.

Gabe gawked at him. "Did you just set your own broken nose?"

Uncle Steve groaned as he got up. "What, you think that's the first time I've picked a fight with a giant mind-reading monster from Arcadia?"

Gabe had no idea whether his uncle was joking or not. Aria still stood nearby, watching them both, her expression calm and unreadable.

Gabe heaved a long sigh. His family was never going to be normal. But they were *his*. He glanced back to where the horrific creature once stood. *And they sure get the job done.*

"Come on," Uncle Steve said, carefully holding a handkerchief to his still-bleeding nose. "We have a breach to find."

As they finally approached the top of the spire, Aria tilted her head up again. "I can feel it." A few minutes later they found another towering set of doors. They shoved them open and stepped out onto the roof of Alcatraz Citadel.

They were so high up, Gabe felt like he was on a plane. The bay below them and the city beyond it looked so tiny, they didn't even seem real.

"Careful," Uncle Steve said. "I can keep the winds more or less under control, but don't get close to the edge."

Aria said nothing. She just glided out toward what they had all been searching for. The breach. A golden crack in the air, about three feet off the ground. Gabe and Uncle Steve trailed after her, and as he got closer to it, Gabe realized he could see the blue sky of home through it.

"This is it!" Gabe felt like laughing. "There's Earth! It's right there!"

Aria circled the breach, calmly examining it, and Gabe's heart plummeted when she reached out and passed her hand right through the gap, as if waving it through a hologram. "It is not a doorway, Gabe," she said dreamily. "You cannot climb through a sunbeam."

The red sky churned angrily overhead.

Gabe turned to Uncle Steve. "What do we do?"

Steve pulled the Mirror Book out of his jacket. As he did, something seemed to catch his eye. "I don't know. But they might." He nodded toward the breach, and when Gabe saw what he was looking at, he let out a whoop of joy.

Gabe might not have been able to cross through the breach, but he could certainly see through it, and there, waving to him from the other side, were Brett, Lily, Kaz, and Jackson. Gabe waved back. "Can you hear me? Guys! Can you hear my voice?"

Lily stepped forward. Gabe's heart did a sort of clumsy backflip in his chest. "We can hear you! Are you okay?" He had to strain to make out her words. It was like shouting down a wind tunnel.

"We're okay! We've got the Arcadia version of the Emerald Tablet. It's called the Mirror Book, and—"

"Gabe, listen!" Kaz bustled up beside Lily. "We're going to try to get you back! We've got the apographon—sort of . . ." He held up the replica's decapitated head. "We're going to try to swap it for you! Okay?"

Gabe wasn't sure how to respond to that, but Kaz didn't give him time.

"Just sit tight, all right? We're still setting up!" He scampered away from the breach, digging around in his backpack. Gabe could see Lily and Jackson helping him, arranging things in a circle.

"Gabe?" Brett stepped forward.

His friend's appearance took Gabe off-guard. It looked like Brett had lost a good ten pounds. His skin had taken on a grayish tone, and there were dark circles under his eyes. But more than that, Brett looked . . . *sad*. Like someone who'd cried so much there weren't any tears left anymore.

"Gabe, I need to apologize to you."

Gabe glanced around. Uncle Steve and his mother stood several paces away, talking quietly, the Mirror Book held between them.

"Don't. Brett, it wasn't your fault."

"But it *was*! I'm so sorry. I'm the one who tricked you all into doing this. I'm the one who got you stuck over there. I started all of this because I was trying to see Charlie again."

Gabe shook his head. "The Dawn sent me here! It wasn't—"

Brett cut him off. "There's more. There's so much more. When I came back, it wasn't *me*. It was Thorne! Jonathan Thorne was *inside* me. Possessing me. He rode me around like—like a freaking bicycle. And I couldn't fight back. I tried, but I just . . . he was too strong. I tried so hard."

Gabe took a step back.

His skin was crawling as if he had ants all over him. *That wasn't Brett with his nose in the Emerald Tablet. It wasn't him putting up that incredible invisibility curtain or getting the apographon to work.* He remembered how suspicious Jackson had been of Brett's abilities, and the skin-crawling sensation got worse. Gabe assumed Jackson had just been jealous, but Ghost Boy had been right. *Maybe Brett* did *do something to the wards at Argent Court to lead the Dawn to us!*

Gabe felt as if he'd just discovered that a stranger had been hiding in the walls of his house, watching him for hours on end. Gabe said, "Holy crap." And when he couldn't think of anything else to say, he said, "Holy crap," again.

"I'm sorry," Brett said.

Gabe didn't think he'd ever seen anyone look as miserable as Brett did at that moment. He tried to put himself in Brett's shoes. It took a little more effort than he wanted to admit. Finally, Gabe made himself say, "Look, you told me yourself. You couldn't fight back against Thorne, right? And you tried. Believe me, I know what it's like to not be in control."

Brett couldn't seem to look Gabe in the eye. "Thorne is here in San Francisco—all of him. He's going to sacrifice everybody in the city, man. Kill everybody in a series of earthquakes, worse than the one in 1906, and then use all those sacrifices at the same time to blow down the walls between here and Arcadia. It's already started."

Gabe's insides dropped into a distant, cold, dark place. *Sacrifice everyone in San Francisco?*

He took another step back from the breach. *All those lives . . .*

They'd talked about the 1906 earthquake in school. He knew how many deaths it had caused. And the city was so much bigger now. So many more people lived there.

And all those deaths would just be a drop in the bucket if Jonathan Thorne actually succeeded in merging Arcadia and San Francisco. Arcadia and *Earth*.

Gabe came to a decision. He knew he had to act on it quickly, because if he spent any more time thinking about it, he'd talk himself out of it. And this wasn't the kind of thing he could let himself get talked out of.

"Brett. Get everybody else where they can hear me."

"But . . ."

"Just do it. Now. Please."

Gabe paced back and forth while Brett called their friends over to the breach.

Lily said, "Gabe? What is it? Did something happen over there?"

Through the breach, Gabe watched the four of them stumble as one, struggling to keep their balance. *Thorne's earthquakes.* Behind them, he saw a tree topple to the ground. He knew the quakes would only get worse.

Unless we finally end this.

Gabe ran his hands through his hair. "Guys. Quit messing around with the apographon. You know the ritual to destroy Arcadia, right? You figured out how to fix it to account for all five elements? Well, you've got to do it. *We've* got to do it. Now. Get it set up, and I'll do my part from here."

Kaz looked as if someone had struck him in the face. Brett turned away, and Gabe thought he saw some tears welling up. Lily shook her head violently. Only Jackson—who met Gabe's eyes for a moment—seemed to understand.

"Forget it!" Words had finally come to Lily. "We can get you out of there! We can *save* you!"

Gabe smiled at her.

After all he had been through. All that his family and friends had been through. It all came down to this one choice, didn't it? Gabe wished he could hold Lily's hand as he spoke.

"I'm with my family. I'm where I'm supposed to be. Don't worry about us." He swallowed hard. "Arcadia's got to be destroyed. It's the only way to save the city—and maybe the whole planet. We're the only ones who can stop Thorne. So let's stop him."

20

Lily watched as Jackson walked Gabe through the ritual. Gabe seemed to understand, and accept, what Jackson was saying.

Kaz was clearly having a harder time with the accepting part. "This is—we can't—" Kaz tripped over his words. "We can't do this! *I* can't do this!" He folded his arms and set his jaw. "I *won't* do this. No way. Forget it."

Jackson finished talking to Gabe and came over to them, but when he opened his mouth to speak, Lily shot him a pointed look and he stayed silent. Lily went to Kaz and put her hands on his shoulders. "Think about what'll happen if we *don't* do it."

Kaz's lower lip trembled. "How can you say that? He'll *die*!

We'll be . . . we'll be killing him! Killing our best friend!"

Lily felt tears well up again in her eyes, but she decided she'd had enough tears. She could break down later. Right now they had a job to do. "Kaz, if we *don't* destroy Arcadia, Thorne's going to smash open the walls between the worlds. Gabe will still die if that happens. *Everyone* will."

She glanced at Brett, hoping for some support, but her brother stood staring at the ground. "Red snake. Red snake. Red snake." He'd been whispering that to himself since he'd finished talking to Gabe.

Kaz sank to the ground and hugged his backpack to his chest. He wasn't crying, not quite, but he rocked back and forth and ground his teeth. Lily knelt beside him, and, to her surprise, Jackson crouched down on Kaz's other side. He looked as if he wanted to help. Lily appreciated it, but she really hoped Jackson's less-than-tactful personality wouldn't end up making things worse.

"Kaz, I don't want to do this, either," Lily said. "I don't want to lose Gabe. I don't want to do this to his uncle or his mom. But we don't have any other choice."

Kaz kept his chin lowered and his eyes closed and didn't say anything.

Quietly, Jackson said, "Kazuo, by deciding to do this we are deciding to save the world. Do you realize that? It is a terrible choice to be asked to make. For us as well as for Gabriel. But we are the only ones who can make it. We five, here in this moment. Kazuo, think of all the families in the city just like yours. All those mothers and fathers. All those younger sisters. No one should be asked to do what we must do now. But the only way to save all those lives is to let Gabriel go."

Now Kaz did start to cry. A low wail escaped him, and the ground around them trembled as green light flashed from between his closed eyelids. He sniffled and looked up at Lily and Jackson. "All right. *Fine*. It's not fair. But all right."

Lily squeezed his shoulder and stood. Brett still hadn't moved, and she went to him. "*Hermano*? Are you still with us?"

Pain clouded Brett's face. "I don't blame you for asking."

"Still can't get this 'red snake' out of your head?"

"Part of the time it seems like a memory, or like I'm having déjà vu. But then other times it's like I've got this *scratch*. On my *brain*."

Lily wanted to help her brother. She did *not* want to have to force a decision on him. Especially this decision. It left a terrible taste in her mouth just to say it out loud. "Brett, if we're really going to do this, we need you."

He rubbed the back of his neck and looked at her sideways. "So that's it, then? There's no other way out?"

"I wish there were another way," she said. "But we can't let Thorne do this to the whole world. Can we?"

Brett shook his head. "No. We have no choice."

As if in response, another violent shock wave made San Francisco tremble. They watched as a tall building across the bay swayed and began to fall. Clouds of dust and smoke turned the air above San Francisco into a thick haze. Lily knew she couldn't possibly hear the screams of pain and fear from this far away, but they were all too easy to imagine. She wondered if there were any people left *to* scream at this point, or if they'd all been encased in blood cocoons.

Brett turned away and hurried to Kaz. Then he, Kaz, and Jackson started preparing for the new ritual. Kaz pulled items out of his backpack, while Brett and Jackson began to add interlocking glyphs of circles and shapes onto the ground. This ritual wasn't that different from the one they had planned to use to rescue Gabe—it would only require a few adjustments.

Lily glanced back at the breach and saw Gabe standing there, watching the whole scene. She went to him.

"I hate this," she called out. Her heart felt constricted, like a wound-up rubber band, and she didn't think it would take much more for it to tear apart. "I want you to be here. I want you to be okay."

Gabe smiled. "I know, Lil, me too. But listen, I have to talk to my mom and Uncle Steve, okay?"

Lily nodded. She couldn't say anything else.

Gabe raised one hand, and Lily tried to press hers against it, but they passed through each other. Matching mirages. Gabe gave her one last look and turned and walked away.

Somehow Lily kept herself together as she turned back to the other boys. Kaz had a notebook and several loose-leaf sheets of paper spread out around him, and Jackson and Brett glanced at them frequently as they positioned small tokens of their elements around the edge of the circle. Kaz concentrated, his slate-gray eyes flashing green. His fingers moved in intricate patterns. Matching symbols carved themselves into the circle at each elemental station. When he was finished, a ring of stone had risen up through the soil, forming a wide circle around the breach.

Jackson caught her eye and came to stand beside her. She said, "This will work, right? Even with Gabe over there?"

"If our research is accurate, I believe Gabriel's participation from the other side will actually strengthen our efforts. We are fortunate that Greta and Dr. Conway had the notion to use Gabriel's mother to the same effect."

Kaz's eyes turned dark again as he looked around at Brett and Jackson and Lily. "I think we're ready. Just one last touch, and then we say the words together."

Lily's stomach tightened painfully. She glanced through the breach, hoping to say at least a few more words to Gabe, but he was too far away, talking with his uncle and his mother. She whispered, "Good-bye, Gabe." Then to Kaz, "Okay."

Kaz carefully took the ring with the Wright family crest and put it on the ground directly below the breach. When it was situated just so, he backed away and held out sheets of paper to everyone. "Here. I've written it down."

Lily took her sheet of paper. She'd seen symbols like these

all over the research notes compiled by Greta Jaeger and Mr. Conway, but never arranged like this. She started to say, "Kaz, I don't know how to pronounce any of this," but as she stared at them, the symbols began to make sense. And the more sense they made, the more it felt as if a swarm of flies had begun burrowing into her brain.

This is the language we heard Primus speaking!

A feeling of dread consumed her.

She glanced up at the breach, and Gabe was back—but not looking at her. Not making eye contact with any of them. Instead, he held what looked like a silver version of the Emerald Tablet.

That's got to be the "Mirror Book" they were talking about. The substitute for the Tablet.

Kaz motioned for them to take their places around the circle. Lily went to hers, and it struck her all over again—the choice they had to make, the loss they were about to face.

Kaz started reading off his sheet.

This is it, Lily realized. Throughout their preparations, she'd known they'd reach this moment when they'd have to say good-bye to Gabe. She still didn't feel ready. But she knew they didn't have a choice.

She joined in, along with Brett and Jackson, and as they spoke in unison, Jackson's eyes turned bright gold. He channeled power out along the circumference of the circle. Connecting them. Boosting them. Brett's eyes shifted to blue-green, and she felt hers phase into silver-white.

From the other side of the breach, Gabe read from the Mirror Book, his clear green eyes replaced by tiny burning stars.

The breach shimmered, wavering. Lily didn't know if that was supposed to happen, but she didn't want to take the chance of interrupting the ritual, so she kept reading. She wished she understood more of the strange, twisted words they were saying.

The ground shook beneath them.

Was that another quake from across the bay?

Kaz's eyes flickered with uncertainty, gray to dark brown and back again, but like her, he kept reading. Lily hated the sound of the Dawn's awful language so much, *so much*, and she wanted to stop, wanted to summon another tornado, a storm so powerful it could rip the breach open and let her bring Gabe and his family through it safely.

She knew that couldn't happen.

Instead, she and her friends were condemning Gabe to death.

She could feel tears building up, pain spearing through her.

Finish the ritual, she commanded herself. *Do it, Lily. DO IT.*

They came to the end of the page. Finally Lily was able to stop talking. The buzzing of flies in her brain died away . . .

. . . and the Wright family ring *twitched*.

The English words feeling oddly unfamiliar in her mouth, Lily asked, "Is that supposed to happen?"

Jackson let the circle of glowing, golden magick fade as he frowned at the signet ring.

Kaz said, "I don't . . . know?"

The ring twitched again, and . . . *uncoiled.*

Brett gasped.

The ring lengthened. Its smooth metal surface grew scaly. Tiny blue eyes appeared, a long, forked tongue flicked out, and the scales turned a deep bloodred.

"Red snake!" Brett screamed. *"Red snake!"* He grabbed at the sides of his head. "That's what I've been seeing! *That's the red snake!"*

The serpent grew, doubling in size in the space of two seconds, and as it coiled on the ground below the breach, it took its tail in its mouth and doubled in size again. *Ouroboros,* Lily thought. A snake eating its own tail—a symbol of infinity. Brett screamed again, and Lily dashed to his side, Kaz and Jackson right behind her.

"Brett!" Lily grabbed her brother's arm and dragged it away from his head. "Brett, what is this? What's happening?"

The serpent kept growing and growing, pulsing on the ground beneath the breach. Gabe was still there, framed in the rip between worlds, shouting something, but she couldn't hear him. Brett stared at the snake in purest horror. "Oh God . . . oh God, I remember now! *I remember!"* He turned to Lily, panic making his voice rise, and grabbed her shoulders. "He tricked us! Thorne! When he possessed me—Lily, it was *his* idea to add the ring to the ritual!"

Jackson pulled Brett around to face him. "What are you saying? What have we done?"

Brett made a strangled sound. "He never had the power to do this on his own! He needed us—*we* had to do it! And he *tricked* us!"

Lily backed away, wide eyes flitting between Brett and the ever-growing red serpent encircling the breach. The golden energy rippling around the breach's edge darkened. Turned red. What was Brett saying? That their ritual—sacrificing Gabe and his family—had *helped* Thorne?

Brett crumpled to the ground. *"I'm sorry!"* he screamed. *"I didn't know—I didn't know!"*

An overwhelming sound filled the air, and Lily sensed it was coming from the serpent. It was a hiss, but it also sounded like the ringing of a bell. Lily *felt* the noise burrow deep into her brain, just like the strange language they'd spoken during the ritual.

The breach became a solid, pulsing ruby red and contracted to a tiny, eye-searing pinpoint of light—before it exploded in a red-gold flash that knocked Lily down as if she'd been hit by a car.

She didn't lose consciousness. Not quite. Vivid red-gold spots floated in her vision, and she knew she'd scraped the skin from her knees and the heels of her hands from the rough, skidding impact. But she thought she must be dreaming. Dreaming or . . .

I'm dead. I'm dead, the explosion killed me.

She had to be either dreaming or dead, because Gabe was there, holding her in his lap, and when the ringing in her ears finally subsided, she heard him saying over and over, "Lily, come back. Lily. Please, please come back."

It took a lot of effort to focus her eyes. "Gabe?"

He laughed. Half relief, half hysteria.

Suddenly very much awake and alert, Lily sprang to her feet and looked around.

The strange red serpent was gone, and so was the breach. Where it had hung in the air, Dr. Conway and Gabe's mother stood. Kaz, Brett, and Jackson were there with them. Lily turned to Gabe, icy fear flooding her insides. She threw her arms around him, but she knew this was no happy reunion. Something was wrong. "Gabe . . . what happened? How are you . . . *here*?"

He pulled away, his green eyes a million years old, and pointed up. "Take a look."

Lily craned her head back and gasped. Huge streaks of amber swirled through the blue and gray sky overhead. She turned around to stare across the bay at San Francisco. As she watched, the Transamerica building grew, twisted, and turned black, until it came to rest as an impossibly tall, malevolent corkscrew against the city's skyline. Other buildings were going through the same strange metamorphosis. Then a flicker of motion pulled Lily's gaze to the Golden Gate Bridge, where she saw a massive swarm of creatures even larger and stranger than abyssal bats. They beat their leathery wings, making their way over the bridge and toward the city. From the waters of the bay, a long, low roar rolled across the waves. It was a sound unlike anything she'd ever heard before, and it froze Lily to the bone.

"Thorne played us," Gabe said quietly at her side. "He made us think his plan was to use the earthquakes and the blood cocoons, but *we* were his real plan all along. The ring he tricked us into using made all the difference."

"What—I don't understand," Lily said. She couldn't get her brain to process what her eyes were seeing.

"Thorne won," Gabe said. "He finally merged San Francisco with Arcadia. Worse than that—he got us to do it for him."

Lily's throat refused to work. She stared out at the city. The city where she grew up. The city she no longer recognized.

The world as she knew it had just come to an end.

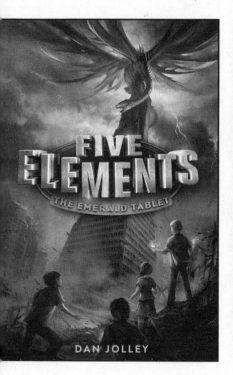